## "Are you in some kind of trouble?" Cade finally asked.

Leah turned away. "Why would you ask that?"

"I don't know. Something about the way you've acted since...well, since I pulled you from the snow. Like you're scared. Why are you in such a hurry to leave? I thought you were staying in the cabin tonight?"

She glanced at him. "I never said I was staying. I asked you to give me a ride back, that's all."

"I just want to help."

Leah sighed. "I know."

"I could take a look at it for you." Now why would he offer that up—an attempt to snag her?

"No." Her reply was too emphatic.

He glanced her way, trying to watch her and the road. To his surprise a timid smile broke through.

"Not tonight, that is," she added. She was trying to be friendly, warm up to him, but still, it seemed forced.

He risked another glance over and caught her eyes— there he saw the truth. She was terrified and hiding something.

*Who are you, Leah Marks?*

**Books by Elizabeth Goddard**

Love Inspired Suspense

*Freezing Point*
*Treacherous Skies*
*Riptide*
*Wilderness Peril*
*\*Buried*

\*Mountain Cove

## *ELIZABETH GODDARD*

is an award-winning author of more than twenty romance and romantic suspense novels, including the romantic mystery *The Camera Never Lies*—winner of the prestigious Carol Award in 2011. After acquiring her computer science degree, she worked at a software firm before eventually retiring to raise her four children and become a professional writer. A member of several writing organizations, she judges numerous contests and mentors new writers. In addition to writing, she homeschools her children and serves with her husband in ministry.

# BURIED

# ELIZABETH GODDARD

HARLEQUIN® LOVE INSPIRED® SUSPENSE

Recycling programs
for this product may
not exist in your area.

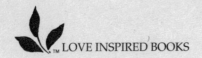

LOVE INSPIRED BOOKS

ISBN-13: 978-0-373-67656-9

Buried

This edition published by arrangement with Love Inspired Books.

® and TM are trademarks of Love Inspired Books, used under license.
Trademarks indicated with ® are registered in the United States Patent
and Trademark Office, the Canadian Intellectual Property Office and in
other countries.

www.Harlequin.com

**Printed in U.S.A.**

This is how we know what love is:
Jesus Christ laid down his life for us. And we ought
to lay down our lives for our brothers and sisters.
—*1 John* 3:16

This story is dedicated to all the true heroes in the world—men and women who risk their lives for other

## Acknowledgments:

It takes many people to write a novel
and I thank my wonderful and amazing family first
and foremost—my husband and children who let me
spend hours far away from them in another world.
Thanks to Shannon McNear—you are always there fc
me! I couldn't do it without you, friend. Writer friend
Kathleen Y'Barbo Miller and Kellie Gilbert assisted n
in figuring out my legal matters. I especially appreciat
the technical expertise from my new friends in Junear
I couldn't have come close to getting things right
without the time and detail they offered. Bill Glude o
the Alaska Avalanche Center, Doug Wessen, presiden
of the Mountain Rescue Association, and my friend
who works for the US Forest Service in Juneau.
If I got anything wrong, that's all on me, but remembe
I write fiction, and I created a whole new town.

# ONE

asping for breath, Leah Marks ran for her life, orking her way through the deep snow from st night's winter storm, the semiautomatic her pocket pressing into her side. What she ouldn't give for a pair of snowshoes.

How had Detective Snyder found her here?

At least she'd seen him from a distance, giving her a few more precious seconds to make a n for it. She had to escape. She wouldn't use er weapon against him unless she had no other oice. Shooting a police detective, even if he as a dirty cop and a killer, wouldn't win her y points no matter which way you looked at it.

Approaching Dead Falls Canyon, she left the ee line and took the biggest steps she could, her ps aching with the effort. She couldn't outrun m this way, but she reassured herself with the ct that he struggled with the same obstacles.

The deep snow would hide the hazards, a Leah counted on that. As she made her wa a snowcapped Mount McCann loomed in h peripheral vision. She'd spent enough time the ski patrol in the Cascades during her colle days to recognize the avalanche risk was high

As she entered the danger zone, a glance ov her shoulder told her Snyder was gaining on h As strong as she was, she couldn't keep up th pace, and as if to confirm the thought, she stur bled headlong into the powder. Leah grapple and fought her way out, gulping panic with ea breath.

With her fall, she'd have to turn and face hi much sooner than she'd hoped. Leaving tow and hiding in an off-grid cabin in Alaska hadr bought her enough time. Hadn't bought h safety.

"Leah!" he called, his voice much too close

Heart hammering, she turned to stand h ground. Stared into his stone-cold eyes. Breat ing hard, he flashed a knife as he approache smirking because he'd finally cornered her.

Dressed to kill, he was in black from head toe—a dead giveaway against the white-carpet mountains.

So that's what death looked like.

Funny that she'd worn white camouflag

oping to remain hidden, for all the good that ad done.

Cold dread twisted up her spine. She thrust er hand into her pocket to reach for her weapon.

It was gone.

No! She must have lost it when she'd fallen. nyder now stood between her and the snow ie'd crushed with her tumble. Between her and er gun.

"Give me what I want, Leah." His dark eyes lashed from the opening in his ski mask.

"Why? So you can kill me like you killed 'im?" She had no idea what Snyder wanted from er, what he thought she had, but she'd witnessed im commit murder. No way would he let her ve.

A thunderous snap resounded above them.

A crack appeared in the white stuff beneath .eah Marks's boots.

The ground shifted.

Before she could react, before she could think, ie avalanche swept her away—swept Snyder way, too—along with everything she'd been aught about how to survive. Carried away by a aunting, crushing force, heavy and swift to kill, he was helpless to stop the power that gripped er with icy fingers.

Roared in her ears.

Terror seized her as the megaton of white

powder ushered her along to a frozen grave, a
untimely death, as though she was nothing mor
than a twig. One brutal way to die had been ex
changed for another.

And then...

Her body slowed before easing to a stop. Th
snow settled and held her inside.

Frozen silence encased her, shrouded her i
muted gray light.

Think. What did she do now? Something
There was something she must do and she mus
be quick. To act before the snow compresse
around her.

Fear temporarily gave way to determinatio
as survival tactics filled her thoughts. She too
in a breath to expand her chest, give her breath
ing room. With her left hand near her face, sh
scooped snow away from her mouth and nos
before it hardened completely. These things sh
did while thrusting her arm toward the surfac
in what she thought was the right direction. I
only she could breach the packed snow and forc
her hand through. Before she could complete tha
one last task, increasing her chance of surviva
it was all over. There was no more give to th
snow—it had locked into place.

Buried alive. She couldn't move.

Icy grayness weighed on her.

She wouldn't dig her way out of this one. Sh

…dn't planned for things to turn out this way. …nic the likes of which she'd never known …oked her, compelling her to gasp for air.

That would kill her faster. She had to conserve …r oxygen.

Inhale…exhale…

Minutes. She had minutes, if that, thanks to …e small air pocket she'd created. She'd been …ven another chance to live, one small chance …a million. Or maybe she would die, but at least …yder wouldn't be the one to kill her.

Calming her breaths, she prayed someone …ould find her in time.

But if that prayer was answered by the wrong …meone…

She was dead anyway.

From the helicopter, Cade Warren stared at the …rtheast face of Mount McCann, struggling to …member the innocence and joy of a carefree …ildhood spent in the mountain's shadow. But …e images from two days ago still haunted him.

Snowboarders out seeking a thrill. Kids who …lieved they were invincible. By the time they'd …lled him to assess the avalanche danger for …search and rescue team, the victims were al-…ady dead.

Beside Cade, his friend and coworker Isaiah

Callahan flew the helicopter deep into the hidden mountain crags.

Cade scraped a hand over his rough jaw. The did more searching than rescuing.

He pushed the thought away, reminding himself that that wasn't what they were there for th time. Today they were supposed to forecast th mountain, assess the avalanche threat in the roles as avalanche specialists.

"I don't get it," Cade said. "Why don't peop read the forecasts?"

"They read them." Isaiah directed the helicopter to the right, angling a little too sharply fo comfort. "They think it won't happen to them

People didn't want to pay attention, which wa why Cade's father had always struggled to ge enough funding for the Mountain Cove Ava lanche Center he'd founded. With his death, h father's frustration had now become Cade's.

The death tolls this week had been bruta making Cade even more determined to do h job. He turned his attention back to the moun tain. In the distance he could see the glacier spilling from the Juneau Icefield.

Strange that in spite of all his expertise, hi father had died in an avalanche, trying to rescu someone. Cade was still trying to make sens of it all.

The one thing he knew was that his father ha

reputation with the town of Mountain Cove as a
al hero—a reputation that Cade strived to earn
r himself. But he doubted he'd ever come close
being the hero his father had been.

"So far we have what—two hundred potential
now slides?" Isaiah asked.

Before he could answer, Cade's pager went
ff. He pulled it from its clip and looked at the
creen.

his is a callout for SAR on an avalanche in
ead Falls Canyon...two victims. Meet at Crank
oint. Respond on Code One frequency...
ase No. 5547.

Cade stiffened. Not another one. He glanced
t Isaiah. "Dead Falls Canyon. We can get there
n time."

His pulse ratcheted up.

Maybe today he could make a difference.

Isaiah grinned his agreement and steered the
elicopter east. First responders rarely made it in
ime to dig someone out of an avalanche. Cade
nd Isaiah were already in the air, near the ava-
anche.

They could serve as the immediate action
eam.

While Isaiah flew them over the harsh winter
errain of the backcountry, Cade communicated

their plans, even as he wondered how and wh
someone would be in the remote area, especial
after last night's storm.

The call had come in three minutes ago. Cad
set his stopwatch to track the critical first fiftee
minutes. They only had twelve left, if the wi
ness had made the call immediately. Cade wer
over a list in his head, glad they always carrie
equipment in the helicopter for such an occasio
Probe. Shovel. And they each wore a transceive
at all times, in case the unthinkable happene
and the helicopter crashed. There was also biv
ouac gear in the event they were stranded on th
mountain.

Maybe today would be the day he could sav
a life instead of recover a body.

Eight minutes.

Cade tensed, praying that the area would b
stable, that he would know where to search. Eve
if they arrived in time, there were safety issue
to consider. They'd need to examine the crow
and path for debris, look for ski poles, glove
goggles—anything that might tell them wher
to look.

Right around the ridge, Dead Falls Canyo
came into view—a deep chasm, rugged an
lethal, in the heart of avalanche country. Cad
tensed at the ominous sight. Breath forced fror

is chest as though he were the victim crushed the slide.

Isaiah sucked in air. "A big one."

"No kidding." Cade looked at the crown where the avalanche began, then down over the resulting debris field. "Six, seven hundred feet wide. Eight hundred long."

"Could be ten, twelve feet deep in some places, Cade. What do you want to do?"

"Get me down there."

"You sure it's safe?"

*Is it ever?* But whoever was buried, if they were still alive, would die if he didn't do something now. He hadn't been there to save his father that day and he'd never forgiven himself.

"I'll take my chances." Five minutes left on the stopwatch.

He swallowed. It could take him longer than that to find the victim much less dig them out.

"Someone's waving at us down there," Isaiah said.

"The witness," Cade mumbled under his breath when he spotted someone layered in winter wear. He wasn't digging, but maybe he could give a few more details about where the victims were last seen on the slope.

"There's no place to land here," Isaiah pointed out, hovering the helicopter over the snow. "I'll need to toe in, touch one ski down while you grab your gear. I'll find somewhere to land, possible, and hike over to help you."

Cade stared at his friend—a man he'd grow close to over the past three years. "Don't set he down. Don't even think about joining me unt you assess the avalanche danger."

Isaiah didn't have a degree in glaciology lik Cade. Didn't have the years of training under mentor like Cade's father that Cade had.

Of the two of them, Cade was far better pre pared—and it still might not be enough. A thirty-three, he didn't have near the experienc or training he needed. He'd lost his father muc too soon.

"Understood?" Cade stared him down.

"Aye, aye, captain." Isaiah saluted him.

Three minutes.

Isaiah touched the helicopter down lon enough for Cade to grab the trauma kit, gea up with his equipment and step out. The land ing zone was tight, and Cade kneeled next t the helicopter, the *whop-whop-whop* of the rotc blades drowning out all other sounds. He gav Isaiah the thumbs-up and watched the helicopte lift off and away.

The witness headed in Cade's direction and in turn, he hurried toward the man, hoping t get the needed information. In the meantime h ırned his beacon from transmit to receive and rayed for a signal.

Cade wanted to know what the witness was oing out here in the first place when the ava-ınche danger was considerable, but there was o time. Two lives were in the balance.

His ski mask hiding everything but his eyes, ıe man pointed to a place between the trees a :w yards away. Not good. "Over there. I think I aw them—a man and a woman—go down, but 's hard to tell where they ended up."

Knowing the range of his beacon, Cade nodded nd hurried to where the man pointed, moving own the center of the debris field, listening, ɔoking for that life-saving signal. And then he ɔcked on to that precious sound.

There was a chance…

He marked the spot.

*Please, God, let me save this one.*

He'd trained for this moment so many times— :arned how to locate a beacon and dig quickly. Ie knew how to assemble his probe without ʻasting precious seconds. But rarely had he had ıe chance to use this particular set of skills with ıe real possibility of finding a survivor.

Two minutes…

Cade hoped to be a hero today, even though e'd never live up to his father's reputation. Pulse ɔunding, he reined in his chaotic thoughts, shut

out the fear and panic. Stayed focused on th
tried-and-true rescue strategies that worked.

Heart bursting, he assembled his probe—a
eight-foot collapsible rod. He drove it into th
packed snow, hoping to feel something—some
one—beneath the surface. He kept searching an
probing until finally the probe hit what felt lik
pay dirt only a few feet down.

A few feet and not ten or twelve or twenty.

*God, please...*

He tossed his probe to the man who'd wit
nessed the avalanche. "Start probing for the othe
victim."

Cade's breath hitched as he thrust the shove
into the snow, hoping he'd made the right dec
sion to send the other man away. Then Isaia
appeared by Cade's side and helped with the dig
ging.

Within a couple of feet they reached a hand

Thirty seconds left on the clock and coun
ing...

Sweat poured from Cade in spite of the cold, i
spite of the fact that he was in top physical cond
tion for his job. Together, he and Isaiah created
tunnel into the snow, searching for the face tha
connected to the hand. No time to stop to chec
for a pulse when seconds counted.

There!

"Establish an airway, stat!"

They dug the snow out and away from the nched features of a young woman so that she uld breathe. Vivid blue-green eyes blinked up surprise and relief, sending his heart into his roat. She was still alive—though he wasn't ne saving her yet. If they didn't free her com- letely and soon, she could still die in her icy rave from hypothermia or internal bleeding.

lso, Cade couldn't forget she hadn't been alone.

"You search for the other victim. I've got this," ade told Isaiah. "I could only get one beacon gnal, though."

"You sure?"

"Yeah. I can dig her out." But he couldn't tol- ate letting someone die when they could save oth victims. Even though they'd passed the first fteen minutes, victims had been known to sur- ive up to two hours on rare occasions. For the rst time in a long time, Cade was on the scene time and every choice he made could save.

Or kill.

Isaiah left his side. From his peripheral vision, ade saw him set his beacon and assemble his robe to search for the other victim. But where ad their witness gone?

Great.

Failing to keep track of the witness would be mark against him within the search and res- ıe team ranks.

No time to worry about him. Cade stare
down into the air tunnel and concentrated o
digging out this survivor—fortunate beyond rea
son—careful to avoid collapsing the tunnel, th
only thing keeping her alive.

# TWO

Leah sucked in a breath, trying to push down the rising panic. Except for her right arm, she couldn't move her body. But at least she could breathe. She blinked up at her rescuer—warmth and respite spilling from his determined eyes, the fierce green of a country spring in the mountains. Streaks of snow clung to his coffee-colored, wavy hair, and though he looked a little rough around the edges, he wasn't Snyder—the man who needed her dead.

Relief filled her and overflowed in an exhale accompanied by a few whimpers. She hated the sound, hated the weakness it conveyed. If she were standing right now, her legs would quiver, unable to hold her weight.

"It's okay. You're going to be fine. I'm digging you out now." Though his eyes held an urgent and untempered concern, his smile reassured her. "My name's Cade, by the way."

That's right, keep talking in those sooth
ing tones.

Cade, wearing the usual thick snow-coun
try gloves, breathed hard as he expertly thrus
the snow shovel in and around her, moving th
iced powder almost as efficiently as a mechan
cal snowplow. He'd uncovered her torso and ha
started digging out her legs.

"What's your name?"

She wasn't sure what name she could trust hir
with. She didn't want anyone to know she wa
here, much less know her name. Telling this ma
could put him in danger, too. She'd been hidin
in the remote wilderness cabin, in fact, whe
Detective Snyder had sniffed her out and com
to kill her. Panic set in and she glanced aroun
at her limited view. Where was he? Had he bee
buried, too?

*Oh, God, please...* But she hated herself fo
wishing him dead.

"It's okay if you're unable to give me you
name," he said.

He probably thought she was in shock. An
she was.

"Is there someone I should call? Friends c
family?"

"No." Her cold answer iced over her heart.
wasn't a lie.

"Can you tell me if you have any pain—how
d it is on a scale of one to ten?"

She felt numb and cold at the same time; stiff,
, though rigor mortis had already set in. Oh,
...was she paralyzed? Had the impact broken
r back?

With the shifting snow she tried to move her
dy. Her legs responded. *Thank You, God.* And
ere wasn't any pain.

"No, I don't think I'm injured. I don't know."
ow could she be sure if something hurt until
e was completely free? She felt so numb, she
uldn't really tell.

His chuckle lightened the seriousness of her
ar death. By the look in his eyes, that had been
s intention. She liked his laugh, but it was hard
trust, even in someone who had rescued her.

"Almost there." He threw the shovel aside and
gan scooping snow away from her back and
gs.

Leah shifted and moved, and the sheer free-
m of that act left her with the daunting aware-
ss that she'd almost died on this mountain
day—twice. The thought pressed in on her,
ffocating her. This man digging her out only
ew the half of it.

As she started to climb to freedom, Cade
abbed her and gently lifted her out as though
e weighed nothing at all. He then set her to the

side, away from the hole that had almost bee
her tomb.

"You sure nothing's broken?" He assessed h
limbs with practiced skill.

Again she moved her arms and legs. "N
nothing's broken. Nothing's crushed inside
I'd be in pain, wouldn't I?"

He pulled something from a pack—a therm
blanket—and wrapped it around her. Crouche
next to her, he wouldn't stop staring at her, unt
finally Leah had to look away.

"You're more fortunate than you know." Th
solemn tone of his voice pulled her gaze up.

She figured he'd ask her why she was skiing
the back country with the avalanche danger hig
but he didn't even ask her what had happened
her skis. She hadn't been skiing, so didn't hav
any, of course, but she had no idea how she'd e
plain her presence here if pressured.

Cade frowned and stood tall, squinting as h
skimmed the slope behind Leah. "What can yo
tell me about your friend? The man you we
with?"

Leah's heart stuttered. She forced a calmne
into her expression she didn't feel. "What mar
I wasn't *with* anyone." True enough.

*What am I doing?* Why lie about Snyder now
Confusion crept over her like the cold trying
slip into the thermal blanket. She wasn't su

ow to handle this. But one thing she felt all the
ay to her chilled core: she wasn't out of dan-
er yet.

Snyder might not be working alone. That
eant she had to stay on her guard and she
ouldn't trust anyone. Until she discovered why
e'd killed Tim that night and what he wanted
om Leah besides her life, she couldn't be safe.
hat meant she needed to disappear again some-
ow. And when she was gone, the less people in
is area knew about her or what had happened
her, the better.

Cade stared down at her, his pensive gaze tak-
g her in once again, wringing her insides as
ough he'd have the truth from her.

"Okay, then," he said. "There was a witness—
meone who'd seen the avalanche and called
in. He reported seeing a man and woman go
der. We have another victim out here some-
here, and I need to help find him. If you think
u're not hurt, and are able, you can search, too.
here's only me and my partner until another
am arrives, but they'll take too long. And our
itness seems to have disappeared after point-
g me in your direction."

What? He had no idea what he asked of her.
ow could she make herself help find the man
ho only moments before had tried to kill her?

Cade must have noticed her reaction. She sa~
suspicion in his eyes.

"Are you okay to rest here, then, while I help?

No. She wasn't okay. She didn't want him t
go. She hadn't felt this safe, this secure, in s
very long. And those things poured from th~
man. She'd never needed that before, and th
realization stunned her. But she reminded he
self she couldn't afford to need anyone. To tru~
anyone. "Sure, I'll be fine."

"Someone will be here soon to evacuate you

Leah nodded and searched the canyon, reliv
ing that moment only a few days ago when De
tective Nick Snyder had shot and killed her bos
Tim Levins, in cold blood.

Tim was a lawyer and Leah was his legal ir
vestigator. She'd been leaving town that nigh
for a three-week vacation. Tim had insisted sh
go and use the bonus he'd given her as thank
for her two years of service in his office. He'
bought her a present, too—a necklace that she'
forgotten on her desk in her rush to put every
thing in order before leaving. She'd stopped b
the office late that night to pick it up, not wan
ing to hurt his feelings if he noticed that she'
left it behind.

Deep down, she knew she had wanted to sto
by the office for more than just the necklac
She'd had a feeling something was wrong…tha

m had been trying to hide things from her.
'd been a little too insistent that she use the
nus to go on a long vacation. So she'd gone
ck to investigate.

She'd liked Tim, but thanks to the trauma
her childhood, she'd never met anyone she
isted, her lawyer boss included.

She'd arrived just in time to witness Tim's
irder. And Snyder—a decorated, trusted po-
e detective and the town's hero—had come
r her.

So she'd disappeared on her own to figure it
out. It had seemed impossible that he'd find
r in the remote cabin hidden deep in the In-
le Passage of Alaska, hundreds of miles from
ncaid, the small town in the Seattle metropo-
where she worked and lived.

Tim had recently inherited the cabin from a
stant uncle. He'd wanted Leah to do some re-
arch for him regarding the man's daughter, who
m thought should have inherited the place. But
woman had vanished. With their case loads,
searching anything about the cabin had been
t on the back burner.

And when she'd known she had to run and
le, the cabin had been the perfect choice be-
use she'd thought no one had known about the
ice or had any reason to connect it to her. That
until she'd spotted Snyder at the cabin.

Until she found out why he'd killed Tim, s[h]
couldn't be sure Snyder had been acting alo[ne]
which meant Leah didn't know who she cou[ld]
turn to with what she'd seen. There could [be]
others in the department who could make h[im]
disappear.

Pulling the thermal blanket tighter, she tried [to]
ward off the double chill that told her she was[n't]
out of danger, even if Snyder died on the mou[n]-
tain today.

Cade and Isaiah were still fruitlessly probi[ng]
for the other avalanche victim when the w[hir]
of an additional helicopter echoed beyond t[he]
spruce trees covered in white icing. The seco[nd]
mountain rescue team had arrived.

He glanced up the hill at Isaiah who gave [a]
shake of his head. By this time, it was high[ly]
unlikely the second victim would survive.

Disappointment corded through Cade a[nd]
pulled tight. He glanced over to where resc[ue]
team members were already preparing to eva[c]-
uate the woman and reminded himself that h[e]
succeeded, at least, in saving her. This cou[ld]
have turned out much differently for her. The[y]
could be placing her in a body bag right no[w]
as they might be doing in a few minutes wh[en]
they discovered the other victim. His chanc[es]
of survival after all this time were almost ze[ro]

ut they would continue the search for as long
; they could safely do so.

Cade's thoughts tracked back to the five snow-
oarding victims.

Five body bags.

Earlier in the week Cade and Isaiah had hiked
ito the backcountry to out-of-the-way paths in
ie higher elevations. On the north ridge they'd
und packed cornices—heavy snow blown in by
ie wind and overhanging a ridge. After dozens
f compression tests to determine the strength
; weakness of the snow layers, Cade had been
ady to call it a week when they'd received the
illout for the snowboarders.

Before the mountain rescue team had even
en able to begin searching for the snowboard-
s, Cade and Isaiah had tossed scores of explo-
ves to trigger the snow that remained above the
valanche—the hangfire snow. Stabilizing the
ea so that the mountain rescue team could go
. All part of their jobs as avalanche specialists.
hat, and forecasting and educating the public.
'hile rescuers had shoveled several feet of snow
uncover the victims, their hapless friends or
mily watching from the sidelines nearly always
ked why this was happening to them.

There was no one standing on the sidelines
day for either this woman or the other victim.
David, Cade's older brother, was leading the

second team. When he spotted Cade, he ap
proached. "Tell me."

Cade pointed to the debris field and explaine
what the witness had said. "We figured wit
the victim's trajectory and where we found th
woman, this would be the likely catchment are
But as you can see, we're still probing."

David grabbed Cade's shoulder. "You di
good, man. You saved someone today. You ca
take that to heart. Now go home and celebrat
We got this. We're already setting up a prob
line and shovel crew. Handlers are bringing th
search and rescue dogs in, too."

As David jogged through the snow to dole o
instructions to his volunteer rescue team, Cad
spotted Isaiah hiking toward him.

"Let's get going. We need to finish our for
casting work before the sun goes down so ther
won't be more victims."

Cade wanted to stay and help. Isaiah must hav
sensed his hesitation. "You're exhausted. *We'*
exhausted. You did what you could, Cade, and
worked. You saved that woman. There are plen
searching for the guy now. Forecasting the ava
lanche dangers, which is your primary job, sav
lives. You can't know how many lives, but yo
have to trust that it does."

Isaiah's words encouraged Cade. His frier
was right. They had work to finish and he'd t

the office until late again, as it was. "I wanted to be more."

"I know you did, man. I know you did. I ⸱rked the helicopter over the ridge. Let's go."

Cade grabbed his gear and followed Isaiah, ⸱dging through the snow that less than an hour ⸱fore had turned brutal and lethal. More often ⸱an not, they had to cart victims—or bodies— ⸱t of the area on snowmobiles and toboggans ⸱cause there wasn't any helicopter access. This ⸱ne they had two helicopters—though Isaiah's ⸱as a single-engine R22—and a survivor. The ⸱22 could only accommodate two passengers,

Cade might have had to wait around or hike ⸱wn on his own while Isaiah evacuated the sur- vor if not for the medevac.

Cade still didn't know her name. Strange that ⸱e'd seemed hesitant to tell him what it was. But ⸱e'd been through an ordeal and he'd given her ⸱e benefit of a doubt.

They topped the ridge and spotted the R22 ⸱d the medevac that provided both medical at- ⸱ntion and transported mountain rescue teams ⸱ necessary.

The woman climbed into the medevac, her ⸱h-blond hair with golden streaks half hidden ⸱der the blanket covering her shoulders. When ⸱d found her, tunneled through to her, he'd been ⸱unned at the blue-green eyes staring back at

him—the crystal purity he'd seen there. Like
tomb raider, he'd pulled her from the snow-lade
crypt and it was then that he'd noticed the re
of her face. She had a clean, natural look. N
makeup hiding flaws. She had an open, hone
look—like someone with nothing to hide.

If only he could believe it were true. She
winced when he'd asked her about the other pe
son with her; denied she'd known anything abo
another victim. She'd been hiding something.

He hated the images that accosted him at th
moment. Images of his fiancée with another ma
They'd been caught in a situation that required
rescue, revealing her deception. Cade had be
devastated that day. Even now his heart was st
too strung out to think about loving again and I
couldn't stop himself from looking at this wom
with suspicion.

Normally he wouldn't concern himself to
much with whether or not someone he'd helpe
was deceiving him. After all, it wasn't as thou
he usually knew any of them well. It wasn't un
a victim teetered on the precipice between th
life and the next that Cade met them, which on
made sense. But then he never saw them agai
He liked it that way. Better to keep his distanc
He'd rescued them. End of story. They did
need him anymore anyway.

His throat twisted tight. He couldn't unde

tand why he didn't want this to be the last time e saw this woman. Then again it had been too ong since he'd rescued someone buried alive in n avalanche. Too long since he'd seen a positive utcome. Maybe that explained it.

With no relatives or friends to call, she had hat proverbial deer-in-the-headlights look about er. Well, who wouldn't after being buried alive? 3ut Cade couldn't shake the sense that she was fraid, scared of something or someone that had othing at all to do with the avalanche.

He had a feeling he wasn't done with this res- ue.

Cade trudged forward and chided himself. He vas probably reading way too much into things. Ie was tired and distracted and too suspicious or his own good. He tugged his gloves off. At he very least, Cade would deliver her home. Vherever that was.

He grabbed Isaiah's arm as the medevac rotors tarted up. "Nothing personal, but you mind if I ide with them?"

"Instead of with me? Thought we were going o finish the assessments?"

"I think we've done all the assessments we're ;oing to do of the mountain today. You have bout enough time before dusk to fly back to the :enter. Anyway, the avalanche gives us a good assessment of the instability. I'll do the report back at the center, so you don't have to."

Isaiah saluted and gave a crooked grin. "Have it your way. So, what *is* your evaluation of the instability?"

"The danger is high."

# THREE

'I need to get a brief medical history, ma'am."
The medic sat next to Leah inside the helicop-
er. "Take your vitals again. They'll do a full assessment at the hospital. Your name and age?"

"Twenty-nine." She didn't want to give her
name; didn't want it surfacing in the computer
system. She wanted to be invisible. To disappear.
"But I'm fine. I don't need to go to the hospital."

He frowned, but didn't push her on that or
her name. He went through a list of questions,
which she answered, portraying a healthy medical history. When he cuffed her for blood pressure, Leah sighed.

*Please, just leave me alone.*

She needed space. Time to think about what
had happened. About what to do next. She in-
haled a breath to calm the turmoil rising inside.

*I'm alive.*

She should be grateful for small things. For
this moment. That she was alive, thanks to God.

And to the man who had believed he'd find someone beneath the snow on a backcountry strip of a lost canyon.

"Looks good." The medic packed his equipment away. "Still, you should go to the hospital for a complete exam. Make sure I didn't miss anything. Internal bleeding or a concussion could be serious."

"Thanks. I'm fine."

He promised to return in a few minutes and hopped from the helicopter.

Maybe he was going to check on the other victim. See if the helicopter was free to whisk her off the mountain. Had they recovered Snyder? Leah's heart stammered at the thought of Snyder, alive or dead. The whole situation filled her with fear.

She strapped herself into the seat, as though it would protect her from whatever would come of it all, the events of the past few hours—past few days—blowing through her thoughts and twisting into a tight knot. For this moment in time—this one moment—she was safe inside this helicopter.

She leaned her head back and closed her eyes.

The deafening whir of the medevac's blades started up. A familiar voice resounded over the obnoxious sound. Leah opened her eyes to see Cade—the man had stepped from her thoughts

to the helicopter. He sent an assessing glance
er way and spoke to the pilot, who nodded.
ade closed the door and took the seat next to
er, strapping in. A few moments later the medic
imbed aboard and sat next to the pilot.

Cade looked at her, that concerned yet calm,
oothing expression she'd seen when he was dig-
ing her out now gone, replaced by something
ne couldn't read. "Hi."

"Hi," she said.

Closing the helicopter's door had turned down
ne volume of the rotors, but not by much. Did
ne relative quiet mean she might have to talk
o Cade? What did he want from her? Had he
eated himself next to her to gather more infor-
nation such as, say, her name? Or for some un-
elated reason?

"You never told me your name."

Leah sighed and looked out the window, away
om him. She would only make him suspicious
f she didn't answer, didn't give him at least this
much of the truth. "Leah. Leah Marks."

She would be forever grateful to him, but she
eminded herself not to take his rescue too per-
onally—that was part of his job. He was likely
volunteer as most were. Men and women from
ll walks of life who gave up their time and their
wn hard-earned dollars to rescue people who

too often made life-endangering mistakes whi
hiking, climbing or skiing.

Her knowledge from her ski patrol experienc
had made her aware of the avalanche risk toda
but she'd had no choice but to run straight int
the danger zone. The way things had unfolde
seemed surreal. The avalanche had prevente
Snyder from harming her.

She wanted to relax and breathe, but sh
couldn't think she was home free yet.

The helicopter lifted up and away. Leah shifte
in her seat to peer out the window, the sun be
ginning its dive toward the horizon. Darknes
would overtake the rescuers soon. Cade leane
over her, a little too closely, to look out the wir
dow on her side. She smelled the faded remnan
of a musky aftershave overshadowed by the ou
doors—evergreens and mountain air and some
thing entirely masculine.

It made her uncomfortable. She wanted hir
to move away.

He pointed out the window. "Look, you ca
see displaced snow from the crown and the patl
That's the avalanche that took you down."

The width and breadth… The whole side c
the mountain appeared to have caved in, fla
tened by snow. Looking like ants from thi
distance, people were searching for the othe
victim. For Snyder.

Her ribs contracted. Feeling her lips tremble, ?ah slid her hand over her mouth. How had ?e ever survived that? She knew…she knew ex- tly how.

She knew exactly who.

Slowly she turned her eyes to look into Cade's. is face was still much too close, making it hard r her to remember to breathe. The burn started :hind her eyes and she blinked at the moisture. at same look of concern she'd seen when he'd rst pulled her from the snowy depths pulsated ?re again.

"Thank you." The whisper creaked from her )s.

His half grin spread wider. "You're very wel- )me."

The sound of his voice was comforting—too )mforting. She knew better than to trust any- ?e, especially now. Besides, men were louses. ?e'd seen the way they'd treated her mother, arning that much at an early age. Every per- ?n was only out for themselves. Even someone ?e Cade.

He eased away from her and Leah breathed ?sier.

"About the other victim, what are his chances?" 'ith this question, Leah's pulse thundered in her ?rs.

She already knew, of course, but she needed

to hear it from Cade. Wanted to know that sl
was at least free from Snyder. And yet part
her knew she should hope and pray he survive
That she could somehow bring him to justic
But the thought of Snyder alive and well, trac
ing her down, plotting the best way to kill h
and leave no trace, terrified her.

Her question had apparently affected Cade,
well. He leaned forward, dropping his head in
his hands. Then, just as abruptly, he sat up, wi
ing them down his face. Obviously losing som
one to an avalanche upset the guy. As though l
felt he was somehow responsible.

Leah didn't know what came over her, but sl
slipped her hand over his. "You did what yc
could. Maybe they'll find him in time." Oh, wl
had she said that?

Though he left his hand in place under her
Cade relaxed his head into the seat back. "H
chances aren't very good. I'm sorry."

He *was* sorry—she could hear it in his voic
see it in his expression.

He didn't know what she knew. The victi
was a murderer. How she hated to see Cade su
fer through the agony of believing he'd let som
one down because he hadn't saved a man toda
Maybe she could ease that pain by telling hi
the man had stalked her, wanted to kill her. The
again, Cade didn't seem like the kind of guy wl

wanted to play God, deciding who should live and who should die.

Regardless of Cade's answer, fear that Snyder or someone involved with him was still out there waiting to kill her clawed across her thoughts.

For a moment Cade had felt like some sort of superhero or something, filled with elation that he'd rescued Leah. Her question had knocked him back to earth.

Leah finally took her hand back from where he'd covered his. Showing him compassion, she'd only meant to help, but she couldn't understand how her simple touch had moved him.

*He* didn't understand it. He didn't want to be moved. Didn't think it could happen.

And then he remembered looking into her crystal-clear eyes from the snow—a life hanging in the balance.

She'd moved him, all right.

For a million reasons he hadn't figured out yet and some reasons he might already know.

He'd been untouchable since Melissa's betrayal. And the pain of his father's untimely death while saving old Devon Hemphill, a man his father had quarreled with for the better part of his life… Cade had no words. Even at the thought of the loss, his heart recoiled.

He stared out his own window now, studying the terrain, looking at the cornices and the buildup of windswept snow after the storms. Al death traps waiting to be sprung. The helicopte carried them away from the canyon and Moun McCann and would set them down at the Inci dent Command Center location.

Leah seemed happy that Cade had left her to her thoughts. She had to be exhausted. Did she have any idea how fortunate she'd been?

God had intervened on this one, Cade was sure. Something Cade rarely saw anymore which made him wonder about God sometimes

"We'll land at the Incident Command Cente for coordinating the avalanche rescue and recov ery," he informed her. "They'll want to take you to the hospital to get things checked out."

She shook her head.

Cade had expected that reaction. "Listen when I was digging you out, you mentioned you had no family or friends for me to call. I need to make sure you get home safely. That is, after your visit to the ER. The hospital staff needs to thoroughly check you out."

"That's not necessary. You don't need to worry about me."

"You might be injured and not even know it."

"The medic already checked me out and said I was fine. I don't need anything else."

Cade knew what the guy had told Leah. Too

ad he was up with the pilot, wearing a headset
nd oblivious to their conversation. Why didn't
he want to go to the hospital? "Look, at least let
ne give you a ride home."

"Thanks, but I can get myself home."

"Really?" Dusk clamping down on them, Cade
hifted in his seat to face her full on. "Because
nless you parked your vehicle at the ICC, you'll
eed a ride somewhere."

Leah blew out a breath. "You're persistent,
ren't you?"

"What kind of rescue is it if you can't get a
ecent ride home?" He was only being courte-
us. That's all this was, wasn't it?

Part of him liked Leah, sure—he'd admit that.
Ie should stay far away from her on that rea-
on alone, except that same feeling came back to
.im that he'd had before. He sensed that some-
hing was terribly wrong. That he shouldn't let
er vanish into the night. He wasn't done with
his rescue.

He almost wanted to roll his eyes at his own
houghts—he thought much too highly of his
bility to assist people.

"Listen, Cade…"

Anything prefaced with those words couldn't
e good. Had he given her the wrong idea? That
ad to be it. But he had a strange feeling that he'd
;iven her exactly the right idea about his inter-

est in her—and he couldn't be interested, not i
that way. How did he protect himself and protec
her? Especially when she clearly didn't want hi
help or protection.

"I'm listening."

"I like you." She paused, appearing to mea
sure her next words. "It's just that I'm not in a
place in my life right now to have friends, espe
cially someone…"

She left the sentence hanging and Cade won
dering what she had planned to say about him
She obviously had thoughts about him one way
or another; she had been thinking about him
Even in the dimming light of day at only fou
o'clock Alaska time, Cade noticed the rush o
color to her beautiful, nature-girl face. He'd be a
jerk if he told her now that he wasn't interested

Cade held up his hands in mock surrender
"Point taken. But I'm only trying to wrap up you
rescue and leave you safe and sound at home. I
not me, then let someone else deliver you there."

Passing her off to someone else to help he
was for the best.

"I'm in a cabin up by Dover Creek. Not fa
from—"

"Dead Falls." Where the avalanche happened
today. "I know the place."

All too well.

After her insistence that he stay out of her busi

ess, he was surprised she'd told him where she
was staying. Acid burned through him. Though
hat explained what she was doing in the ava-
anche area, it didn't explain why she was in
ld Devon Hemphill's abandoned cabin. When
Devon had died not long after Cade's father had
saved him, he'd taken with him the chance for
Cade to get answers to his questions as to why
his father had given his life to save the man he'd
always seemed to hate. Could the answers be hidden somewhere in that cabin? Was he supposed
o meet Leah for that very reason?

"You said there was a witness who called to
et you know about the avalanche." Her shaky
voice weaved through his tumultuous thoughts
and pulled him back to the present.

"Hmm?" He turned to face her again, her ques-
ion sinking in. "Yeah. He pointed to where he'd
seen you and the other man, and that helped me
o pinpoint where to search for a beacon signal."

Which reminded him. "You wore a beacon.
Smart girl. But you weren't wearing skies or
snowshoes, unless the snow slide stripped them
rom you." He was probing, now, hoping she'd
ell him why she'd been out there. People didn't
usually hike or ski the backcountry in the winter
alone. It was stupid and dangerous, even if she
was staying in a nearby cabin. She'd told him
hat she didn't know the victim, so why had she

been out there alone? For that matter, why woul
the other victim be out there alone?

Things didn't add up. Her story didn't fi
Maybe it wasn't his business, but he wanted t
know what she was hiding.

"What else did he say?" She frowned.

Why would talking about the witness make he
frown? Without that guy's efforts, she wouldn'
have survived.

"His call about the avalanche and the infor
mation he gave us saved you. I guess you coul
say he was the real hero today, whoever he was,
Cade said. "After he pointed me in your direc
tion, there wasn't time for much small talk.
asked him to help find the other victim, bu
by the time my partner got there, the man ha
bailed."

"What did he look like?"

Cade stared, wondering why it mattered, i
she'd been there alone as she'd claimed. Hadn'
seen anyone else, as she'd said. What was sh
digging for? Her questions spiked Cade's curi
osity even more.

"The witness," she said again. "What did h
look like? What was he wearing?"

He scratched his head. "Black. Everythin
black, including his ski mask. I could only se
his eyes."

Fear rippled across her face in a quiet shudder

# FOUR

*He survived.*

Everything tilted. Leah gripped the seat, unsure if Cade's unwitting confirmation that Snyder had been the "witness" had sent her world spinning or if the helicopter had simply angled sharply.

Or did he have a coconspirator? She doubted that, whatever he was up to, he was working alone. It seemed too hard to pull off a cover-up as a detective without someone else watching your back. But that remained for her to investigate. Before today, she had seen no one else at the cabin. No one other than Snyder had pursued her. Unless there'd been someone else dressed exactly the same that happened to be in a position to witness the avalanche and make the call. That would be far too coincidental.

Pulse throbbing in her neck, Leah looked out the window and away from Cade. He was too

perceptive and would see her distress. She'd hel
on to a sliver of hope that Snyder had been burie
in the avalanche today. That would have at leas
bought her time to investigate, discover why Tin
had been murdered and who else, if anyone, wa
involved, before she went to the authorities—th
ones she could trust, anyway.

But now...she'd have to keep running for he
life. Her nightmare wasn't over, not by a long
shot, and she doubted Snyder would give he
much time before his next attack.

Images of him killing Tim in cold bloo
flashed through her thoughts. His words re
sounded in her head. "Give me what I want
Leah."

He'd called for a rescue team. That he neede
her alive was obvious. She'd thought he only
wanted to kill her because she'd witnessed Tim'
murder, but his words on the mountain told
much different story.

No. He needed something from her first and
then he'd kill her. An image of his knife flashe
in her mind. Leah shuddered.

"Are you okay?" Cade asked.

What should she tell him? What explanatior
could she possibly give? The truth wasn't an op
tion.

"Leah, is everything all right?" he asked again

Leah rubbed her arms. "I'm fine." The events of the past few hours played through her thoughts, images of her icy tomb wrapping around her once again.

She'd come here to hide, to stay alive, to investigate Tim's murder from a safe distance. But now she had to add one more thing to that list: finding out what Snyder wanted from her.

Thankfully, Cade seemed to sense her need to process everything because he didn't ask more questions. The helicopter landed and Cade assisted her onto the pavement of the parking area swarming with emergency vehicles with flashing lights.

A rescue worker approached Cade. "A storm's moving in."

Cade frowned, eyeing Leah. "They're giving up the search for the other victim then?"

"The incident commander suspended the search. He'll reevaluate at first light," the guy said, then left Cade alone with Leah.

"There's no point in risking more lives." Cade's intense gaze studied Leah. "Unless they found something to indicate they were close to finding him. Skies, gloves or poles. Something like that."

Her throat constricted. Shouldn't she tell him that there wasn't another victim? Except, what if she was wrong? What if Snyder *had* been buried in the avalanche? The witness had said there were two people who had gone down in the avalanche. If Snyder had survived and made that call, then why would he lie about the number of people needing rescue?

To throw her off? Maybe he believed that if she thought he was dead, she'd let down her guard so he'd have the advantage again. Leah wrapped her arms around herself, wishing she could tell Cade everything. But it wouldn't help—they would still need to search for another possible victim if there was any chance someone was still trapped out there. Besides, she couldn't tell anyone about her predicament. Not until she knew who she could trust.

Dropping her hands, she eyed the man who had pulled her out of the snow. He hovered over her as though he was afraid to let her out of his sight.

She didn't need some overprotective rescuer getting involved in her life, putting himself in danger for her any more than he already had.

She needed to find a way to get her things from the cabin and get out. But as Cade had pointed out, she didn't have her vehicle. It was parked in the shed at the cabin along with a snowmobile. Besides, the road would be treacherous and maybe unnavigable in the dark with the storm moving in.

At least Tim had paid some guy to keep the drive to the cabin plowed. There was only one way in and one way out and considering she had a killer after her, she liked it that way. But now that her hiding place had been discovered, she couldn't afford to stay there.

"If you're still willing to give me a ride back to the cabin, I could use that."

He nodded, as if he'd only been waiting for her to see the obvious. "I know the road well. I can get you there."

"I appreciate your help." She hung her head. "I hope it's not too much trouble."

"I like to finish the job. Make sure you're safe and secure, tucked away at home. The only problem is that with the storm coming in, I don't know if that cabin is fully secure. You sure it's a safe place to stay?" He lifted a brow.

No. But not for the reasons he might think. She held her hand to her forehead. "Look, I'm tired. I need to get back." She wouldn't call it home. Leah couldn't return to her real home—a small apartment a few miles from Tim's office. But one thing at a time. One day at a time. She had to survive this night first.

"Okay, then." He watched her for a few seconds longer than necessary. What was he thinking? Then he turned his attention to finding a ride. He spoke with a police officer, and Leah stiffened. She turned away, concealing her shudder. Snyder had driven home her reasons to fear people who were sworn to protect. But then, her past had already done that for her. She'd watched helplessly from the sidelines as people sworn to protect had put an innocent woman in prison. Put her mother in prison.

Someone agreed to transport Cade and Leah to Cade's vehicle. From there, he could take her to the cabin. She climbed into the backseat of the sedan, while Cade sat in the passenger seat. He and his buddy spent the drive talking about the avalanche. They didn't engage her in their conversation, which was just as well. But she knew that wouldn't last. Cade was all too clearly the inquisitive type. She couldn't really hold it against him—she was the same way. It was one small part of why she'd become an investigator. But any digging that Cade did into her situation was only going to cause trouble for them both.

Once Cade got her alone, she had a feeling his interrogation would start. He was perceptive, and she'd read in his eyes that he had questions. She wasn't sure how to evade them, but she had to try. She hadn't done a good job of hiding her emotions, but maybe she could convince him that her state of mind was all due to the avalanche. Involving someone else in her dilemma, possily putting them in danger, wasn't something he would willingly do.

Leaning her head against the headrest, she closed her eyes. This brief respite, this was the first time in hours she could shut off what was going on around her, if only for a few moments, as Cade and his friend talked about the approaching storm. Another one. She thought that southeast Alaska, with the temperate rainforest, was supposed to be milder than interior Alaska. Maybe it was—but it sure didn't seem that way to her.

Ignoring the words, she let Cade's smooth voice wrap around her again, reminding her of when he'd spoken reassuringly to her as he'd dug her out. She couldn't ignore that the whole rescue-hero thing was more than attractive. Add to that, the guy seemed so selfless. His concern for her, when he had no reason to care about her at all, was disconcerting. So unlike any of the men she'd known. But there had to be some reason she couldn't trust him. Even if she didn't know it yet, she'd find it. Men couldn't be trusted—her boss and trusted hero Detective Nick Snyder were prime examples. This Cade guy had a secret, a side to him he kept well hidden.

Everyone did.

They arrived at the avalanche center, which shared space with other businesses in a five-

story building along the main thoroughfare in
Mountain Cove. Cade and Leah got out, and
Cade thanked the guy for the ride before lead-
ing Leah to his vehicle.

It was only four-thirty in the afternoon in Feb-
ruary, and the sun was already setting. She'd
only had three days at the cabin, but had learned
quickly how limited the daylight hours were in
the dead of winter. Parking lot lights illuminated
Cade's big blue truck sitting at the side of the
building along with other vehicles. But his was
the only vehicle with a plow attached to the front.

She glanced at him and he shot her a grin. "I
live up a long drive. It's a little higher elevation
than the town, and snows a lot more."

Leah couldn't help herself. She smiled back,
the first genuine smile to cross her face in days.
But she couldn't let herself get too comfortable
with him. She needed to vanish. Once he took
her to the cabin, she could pack her stuff and
leave.

Disappear.

If only there was another place on earth farther away than a lone, off-grid cabin in Alaska.

Sitting in the warm cab of his truck, Cade
glanced at his passenger. He hated the awkward
silence, but what had he expected?

Snow filled his headlights as he drove away

rom Mountain Cove on the one road out of town. The only problem was that the thirty-mile road idn't go anywhere. Just came to an abrupt end. To say the town was isolated was an understatement, but this was southeast Alaska where "remote" took on a whole new meaning. The only way in and out of Mountain Cove was by boat, floatplane or helicopter.

At least Cade could get to the road to Devon's cabin this way. Accessing most off-grid cabins required serious trekking by snowshoeing, skiing or snowmobiling for miles.

Up in the mountains, sometimes even the cabins got buried in the snow. That's why uncertainty about Leah's stay in the place gnawed at him. Devon had known how to dig himself out of the snow up there, but Leah looked like anything but a mountain girl.

It didn't help that his protective instincts had picked up a few notches after he'd pulled her from the snow, and they hadn't shut down. No. In fact, if anything, the thought of her staying in that cabin in the heart of avalanche country—especially with another storm rolling in—put his protective instincts on high alert.

He reminded himself he didn't know enough about her to make that kind of judgment call. She might be completely capable of handling a stay

at the cabin during a harsh winter—and this on
was certainly looking that way.

"You warm enough?" he asked. "Need mor
heat?"

"No, I'm good. Thanks."

That was all she said. His neck tensed. Hov
did he get her talking? He wanted her to open u
for a lot of reasons. For one, he wanted to knov
what she'd been doing out there today. She'd al
most died. The panic and fear he'd seen in he
eyes was because she'd been shell-shocked fror
having barely survived an avalanche. But th
natural disaster didn't explain all of her reac
tions. When she'd asked about the witness, an
he'd told her, she'd all but freaked out. He'd see
her eyes before she'd turned her face from hir
in an attempt to hide her reaction.

What was that about? Cade couldn't shake th
sense that she knew something vital she had n
intention of sharing.

He pursed his lips and watched the road, th
glow of the dash lights contrasting to the dark
ness outside. He had to be honest with himsel
Sure, he wanted to help her, but he also wanted t
know whatever Leah could tell him about Devo
Hemphill and why she was in his cabin.

More than anything, he wanted answers to th
story behind his father's quarrel with the mar
He wanted answers to explain the reasons behin

his father's tragic death. Those were answers he doubted he'd ever get. But he had to try. Leah might know something. She might be able to give him a clue.

When Cade finally made the turnoff to the cabin, he was surprised to see the drive had recently been plowed, but snow was already piling up again. He glanced at Leah. Maybe she was more capable than he'd given her credit for. Still the new snowfall would make the drive long and tedious.

He stopped.

"What are you doing?" she asked.

"Have to engage the plow." He climbed out, lowered the blade and then got back in the truck, Leah watching him.

"So, I knew the guy who used to own the cabin where you're staying. Devon Hemphill. You related to him or something?"

Leah stiffened and grabbed the armrest. Whether from the question or the slipperiness of the road, he couldn't tell.

"A friend inherited the place. They are letting me stay for a little while."

Cade glanced over again. A friend, huh? She conveniently left off if the friend was male or female. Not that it mattered to him. All he cared about was finding answers to his questions and making sure she was safe. He had a feeling, a very strong feeling, her life was in need of rescuing again. Cade scraped a hand down his face—was he even up to that task?

More importantly, did it matter if he wasn't up to it? He couldn't abandon someone who needed help. He just wished she'd tell him what was going on. Maybe if he gave up something private and personal, she would, too. Reach out to her and then she'd reach back. He could pull her the rest of the way.

*What are you doing?*

"Devon Hemphill and my father knew each other well." Maybe a little too well. "They had an ongoing disagreement about something. I never could figure out what. It seemed to escalate as the years went by."

He'd tried to ask about it so many times but all his father would tell him was to mind his own business. Completely out of character, considering Cade and his father were close. So Cade had tried to learn more by digging for answers in other ways, but none of them had panned out. "My father and I argued about that the day he died."

"I'm sorry," she said.

He waited, hoping for more.

"I didn't get the chance to say anything else to him before he got the call for a search and rescue. Didn't get the chance to say I was sorry."

He kept his eyes on the road, reliving that day. In his peripheral vision he saw Leah watching him, waiting for the rest of the story. He wasn't sure he could keep going, especially with a perfect stranger. But maybe that was exactly the person he could tell, say it out loud to. Face his battles head-on.

"The stranded person was Devon."

Leah gave a slight gasp. "What happened?"

"I never saw my father alive again. Devon walked away and my father died during the rescue mission to save that man. A man he detested. I still don't understood why." Cade blinked back the memory of pulling his father's body from the avalanche and pushed the rising anger down. "My father liked everyone, and was liked by everyone. Except Devon."

He felt as though he'd said too much. But maybe in the telling he could stir things up and get information. "I never got an answer from Devon about what had happened between them, and then he died, leaving me with nothing but questions."

"Now here I am, staying in his home," she said.

Cade didn't reply. It was her turn to talk.

When the truck's high beams illuminated Devon's cabin in the distance, Cade thought he saw someone in the trees behind the pile of old tires

and barrels of diesel for the generator. Had to b
the shadows dancing off his lights. Who woul
be out here at this hour in the middle of nowhere
especially with a storm moving in? Unless Lea
wasn't alone in the cabin. But that couldn't b
the case, could it? She'd told him there was n
one he could call.

Stopping the truck at the end of the drive, h
shifted into Park but left the motor idling. A so
glow emanated from one of the cabin window;
At least she wouldn't have to enter a completel
dark house, although she'd have to hike the fin;
twenty-five yards. He couldn't get the truck be
tween those trees.

"And here we are at Devon's once-empty cabir
now your vacation home away from home." H
repeated what she'd said earlier, thinking tha
might ignite more conversation on the topic. H
hid a wince at the sound of his own gruff ton(
which had been way more accusatory than he'
intended.

"Look, I didn't happen upon the cabin and fin
it empty and decide to stay."

Yeah, she'd heard it in his voice, too. "I didn
mean to insinuate otherwise." He blew out
breath, hoping she understood. "Thinking abou
everything that happened frustrates me in way
you can't understand."

"You're wrong. I do understand. You blam

ourself for your father's death. You think you
ould have been with him that day."

Cade nodded, surprised at her words. "If I had
een, maybe he would still be alive."

"Or maybe you would have died instead." She
ared at her hands in her lap. "I know how you
el. I have my own regrets. Things I wish I had
one differently. But we can't change the past."

"No, we can't."

"I can't help you find the answers, Cade, if
at's what you're thinking. My friend who in-
erited the place never said anything about the
an who used to live here. I'm sure he…doesn't
now. But I'm sorry you lost your father. I'm
ure he was very proud to have a son like you."

Her words were clearly meant to heal and reas-
ure, but instead they scraped across his wound.

"I don't know."

Cade strived to live up to the kind of man his
ther was, but always felt as if he fell short. An
wkward silence filled the cab again. He'd got-
n too personal.

She clutched the door handle, glancing back at
ade. "Thank you for saving me today and for
inging me here."

"Wait," he said. "Are you sure you should stay
re by yourself after the rough day you've had?
specially with the storm coming?"

"I'll be fine, I promise." Something contrar
to her words flashed in her eyes.

Cade was skeptical, but what could he do? "I'
come in and get the fire stoked."

He shoved on his door and the cold air blaste
into the cab of the truck, swirling icy snowflake
around them.

"No," she said, the force of her words mear
to convince. "No, Cade. Please, go home. You'v
done enough."

Cade nodded reluctantly, recognizing whe
he'd been dismissed. He shut the door as sl
opened hers and stepped out.

Headlights illuminated the cabin while he con
tinued to wait, thinking he'd watch her go safe
inside. For the longest time, he'd been about sa
ing people. She might have sent him away, b
the anxiety lurking in the shadows of her blu
greens said she still needed his help.

How could he turn his head now? As long a
he could keep his heart in a safe place.

Out of danger.

# FIVE

is intense gaze softened, the accusation gone—
t not forgotten. Though he came across as con-
rned and protective, she knew he didn't trust
r. But he didn't have to. This was where they
ent their separate ways. Still, Cade made her
sh she could trust people. Trust men. This one
particular. Take his help instead of going into
at cold cabin alone. Even if she trusted him,
e didn't want to pull him into the danger that
as closing in around her. Smothering her more
ickly than she ever imagined.

How could she live with herself if something
ppened to the man who had saved her today?

"Goodbye, Cade." She slammed the truck door
d stepped into knee-high snow covering the
th to the cabin.

Arctic cold swirled around her, chilling her to
r bones despite her parka and down bib over-
s, and stirring doubt deep inside about her next
ove. She hurried by the wood pile and chop-

ping block, glad she'd already stacked more fir
wood next to the cabin door. Yet another thin
that didn't matter—she wasn't staying the nigl

Snyder knew where she was hiding. He'd ma
his way back as soon as he thought it was sa
and that meant her time was running out. Was
already there, inside the cabin, waiting for he
There was no way to tell. The headlights fro
Cade's truck kept the cabin in the spotlight a
for that she was thankful. She'd told him to lea
but as she closed in on the cabin, she wasn't su
she'd made the right call.

Why couldn't Tim have inherited a hut or
tropical island? She made her way to the do
and paused. What would she find inside? Wou
the place be torn apart, her stuff scattered e
erywhere because Snyder had come to find h
and whatever he thought she had? One thing s
knew, she hadn't had a chance to lock up befc
leaving earlier. She'd gone to explore one of se
eral small buildings on the property and wh
she'd returned, she'd seen Snyder step out of t
cabin and lock eyes with her.

At the memory, a shudder ran over her. Hc
had Snyder located her? Whatever it was th
had given her away, another mistake like th
one could be deadly.

Taking a deep breath, she shoved the door op
and stepped inside. Nothing appeared disturbe

nd that confused her. But she could figure it all
ut after she gathered her things.

She wouldn't be here long enough to bother
ith stoking the fire, but the cabin was well in-
ulated and remained relatively warm, consider-
ng she still wore her parka.

The kerosene lamp in the corner hissed, crack-
d and dimmed. Leah quickly added more fuel,
rightening the small living area, shadows blink-
ng in the tiny bedroom and the mudroom. Grab-
ing the lamp, she carried it into the mudroom
 chase the darkness away from the shelves and
e solar energy equipment, making sure she was
lone.

When she'd first arrived, it looked as if Devon
ad been experimenting with solar power even
ith the limited sunlight in this region. But Leah
ad used the lamps and generator for the short
ime she was here. The oil stove in the corner
aught her attention—she could use some cof-
ee or hot tea after the day she'd had, but she
idn't have time for that. On the kitchen counter
y the knife she'd used to cut an apple earlier
hat afternoon. It reminded her of when Snyder
ad flashed a knife at her today. She'd lost her
andgun this afternoon, and would need another
veapon.

Leah grabbed her laptop from the table. Had
Snyder searched her files? Could be that was

why he hadn't bothered ransacking the cabin
He wouldn't have found anything. For all her in
vestigative prowess, Leah had failed to get the
one photograph that would change everything
The photograph of Snyder murdering Tim in col
blood.

An image forever seared in Leah's mind, fo
all the good that did.

And that's why she understood Cade's anguis
and self-recrimination—that feeling he seeme
to carry that if there was anyone Cade shoul
have been able to save, it was his father.

And if Leah couldn't save Tim that night, a
least she should have taken that photograph.

Had she not been paralyzed where she'd stoo
and instead taken the picture, Snyder would hav
been quickly put away with the evidence again:
him. She could have gone to the press or poste
it on the internet for the world to see so tha
Snyder or his coconspirators couldn't bury th
evidence. Without it, no one would believe he
against a town hero and decorated police offi
cer. Snyder was free to stalk and kill her, muc
as he was doing now.

If she hadn't seen it with her own eyes, sh
wouldn't have believed it—his actions were com
pletely out of character with his public image
He must have been desperate to commit murde

ow he was desperate for something from her—
d he was clearly willing to kill again.

After stuffing her laptop into her briefcase,
e carried the lamp to the bedroom to grab her
ffel bag and pack her few belongings inside.

A sound stopped her. The back door? Panic
gulfed her.

Was it Snyder? She stood stock-still.

Listening.

In this case, the light wouldn't chase the mon-
ers away. Leah snuffed out the lamp. Keeping
er location obscured was her only chance to get
way if someone had broken in.

Utter darkness wrapped around her. Her heart
ounded, needing escape.

Now she wished she had asked Cade to wait.
he could have followed him down the moun-
in in her own vehicle. If only she could have
ld him everything.

The floor creaked somewhere in the inky
ackness of the cabin. Near or far she couldn't
ll. Holding her breath, she listened to the foot-
lls that let her know she wasn't alone.

They grew closer, permeating the small dwell-
g with deadly tension. Fear surrounded her like
undreds of snakes slithering over her body,
round her neck, arms and legs, paralyzing her.

The knife on the counter. If only she'd taken it

the moment she'd seen it. If she could make h
way to the kitchen.

*Move. Your. Legs.*

Leah's breathing ramped up. She was tough
than this. *Do something! Save yourself!*

"Leah." It was Snyder. His voice was low ar
threatening. "This can all be over. You can hav
your life back. Or disappear, I don't care. B
give me what I want."

Liar. He'd killed Tim and would kill her, to
She wanted to tell him that, wanted to ask hi
what he thought she had, but said nothing. In th
blackness, answering would give her positio
away. Instead, she stood in her prison of dar
ness and listened to his deadly threats.

Cade had only driven a short distance whe
he decided to wait and watch for a few minute
in his rearview mirror, unsure of what he woul
see. Maybe he was crazy, but he kept thinkin
about the moment when he'd first driven up. H
thought he'd spotted something in the shadow
but at the time, he'd disregarded it. Cade didn
like that Leah was staying in the remote and il
fitted cabin to begin with.

And suddenly, the place went dark. Completel

Leah was probably tired and had gone to be
early, and he was an idiot. If she knew he was ou
here, she'd think him a stalker. But hadn't she

ast stoked the fire? If she had, Cade would be ble to see the dim light through the windows. he couldn't blame him for checking on her. A erson could die up here if they didn't know what they were doing. He should have insisted n going inside and stoking the fire. Check on hings. He reminded himself that Leah was a rown woman perfectly capable of taking care f herself. She'd made it clear she wanted her rivacy.

Perfectly clear that she didn't want his help. Didn't need him to rescue her.

Yeah, yeah. None of that eased his gut feeling—a feeling he'd learned to listen to when it ame to avalanches, when it came to search and escue. And he couldn't ignore it now. He steered he truck in a U-turn on the narrow drive, tires pinning and grinding through the deepening now. Cade would never forgive himself if he idn't at least check on her one last time. Staying n the safe side was worth the risk of her thinking him an idiot any day of the week.

Hand lifted to knock, he stood at the door. All was quiet inside. Almost too quiet. Should he orget it and leave her alone? Except, he knew he lights from his truck would have disturbed er already.

He blew out a foggy breath. Here went nothing. He pounded on the door. "Leah, it's Cade."

Three seconds went by before the door flew open and Leah rushed out. He caught her in his arms, buffering the sure collision. Gripping her shoulders, her face near his, he witnessed the fear in her eyes before she pulled away.

"What's wrong?" he asked.

"I need a ride down the mountain, after all. Can we get out of here?"

"Of course."

Leaving him behind, she hurried for his truck, carrying bags, trudging over the snow-covered ground like a fugitive fleeing in the night. This was getting weird. He was glad he'd hung back and waited. Glad he'd decided to check on her. He only had a degree in glaciology but it didn't take a rocket scientist to see something was wrong. Just as he suspected this afternoon as he'd watched her. Just as his gut told him while sitting in the truck. But what the problem was... he didn't know.

He glanced back through the door she'd left open, seeing nothing inside the cabin except darkness reaching out to him, and raising the hairs on his neck. Was it only his aversion to all things Devon Hemphill and the memories that accompanied him, the cabin included, or was there truly something sinister inside?

He shut and locked the door then hurried after Leah. She was already sitting in the truck. Cade imbed in on the driver's side and studied her, oping she'd tell him what was going on, but he didn't even look at him. She wasn't wearing loves and her hands trembled. From the cold or omething else? Cade had thought she was stay-ig in the cabin, but a duffel bag and briefcase sted in her lap.

"I'm glad you came back to check on me." er voice cracked. "But it's getting late. Snow-ig hard. Can we go?"

Cade frowned, disturbed to his core. The nowplow still engaged, he shifted into Drive nd headed back to Mountain Cove. He'd ask her here she wanted him to take her, but there was nly one way back to town and he had a more ressing question.

Tense and breathing a little hard, Leah kept lancing in the side mirror.

"Are you in some kind of trouble?" he finally sked. Might as well get right to the point.

"Why would you ask that?"

"I don't know. Something about the way ou've acted since…well, since I pulled you from ie snow. Like you're scared. Why are you in ich a hurry to leave? I thought you were stay-ig in the cabin tonight."

She huffed a laugh. "I didn't mean to mislead ou. I never actually said I was staying tonight, just that I would be fine. I asked you to give me a ride back, that's all."

"Well, I must have misunderstood. It's none of my business if you stay. I just want to help."

Leah sighed. "I know. As for me not staying here tonight, the cabin isn't completely functional yet. I needed to grab my things, and with the snow really coming down, I realized I'm not sure I can make the drive down. I don't have the plow like you do. I made a mistake in ignoring your concerns to begin with."

Her words made sense but Cade had a feeling they were only for his benefit, and meant to hide something else. His brothers would want to knock him in the head for digging into her business like this. For not taking her words at face value. And as for driving back to town tonight in the storm, Cade had a feeling she would have tried if he hadn't been there.

"I could help you attach a plow, if you want. They'd have to order one from Cooper's in Juneau to fit her specific vehicle.

"No." Her reply was too emphatic.

He glanced her way, trying to watch her and the road. To his surprise a timid grin broke through.

"Not tonight, that is," she added. She was trying to be friendly, to warm up to him, but still it seemed forced.

He risked another glance over and caught her yes—where he saw the truth. She was terrified nd hiding something.

*Who are you, Leah Marks?*

She was in trouble.

He wanted to protect her from whatever evil vas after her. Protect her even from trouble of er own making, if that turned out to be the case. Ie hated himself for that innate instinct that was n his blood, but as long as he kept his heart out f it, he should be safe.

He concentrated on the road and the driving nowfall, growing thicker by the minute. One vrong move on his part and they could end p down an embankment stuck in the snow or vorse. When he made it to the intersection with ne highway that led to town, he slowed to a stop t the sign.

"Where to?" he asked.

"What?" She turned from staring out the pas-enger window, the look in her eyes telling him er thoughts had been a million miles away.

"You left the cabin," he said. "Where were you lanning to stay?"

"Could you recommend a quiet, out-of-the-vay motel?"

Cade rubbed his scruffy jaw. Sure, he could hink of a few. Mountain Cove might be out of ne way and hard to get to, but people came from

all over to hunt and fish and get away. The tow
counted on that money. There was a bed-and
breakfast, too, but it might be booked up. Hi
family was friends with the owner, Jewel. Cad
could give her a call. But another thought bu
rowed in as if coming in from the cold. "I hav
an idea."

Troubled eyes gazed into his. Strength, dete
mination, the will to survive lingered in ther
as well. She blinked, waiting for him to go on.

"You could stay with my grandmother and sis
ter tonight. Then figure things out tomorrow."

"I couldn't do that."

"No, really, you can. My grandmother woul
want me to invite you." Especially under the ci
cumstances, though he wasn't exactly sure wha
the buried details of the circumstances were. Bu
that shouldn't matter. Leah was in trouble, an
he knew without having to ask that his grand
mother would want to help.

Cade turned onto the road and headed home
wondering if she would take him up on his offe
He hoped so. Leah could use the kind of nurtu
ing only his grandmother could give. She'd com
to live with them after his mother died twent
years ago. Cade had been thirteen then, hi
brother David, seventeen, Adam, ten and Heid
eight. His father had been devastated after losin
his wife, and caring for four kids while workin

asn't an easy task. The arrangement had been ood for Cade's grandmother, as well.

"Come on," he cajoled. "It's a cold night. ou've been through a lot today. Grandma cooked p a nice big pot of beef stew and homemade olls."

Leah's stomach rumbled. Cade almost laughed t that, but he kept it inside.

She quirked a brow. "You're not playing fair. Besides, how do you know what she cooked? ou've spent what feels like the entire day res- uing me."

"I know because she told me this morning hat she'd be making. She and Heidi, my sister, now I can't always make it in time, but they eep the food warm. Just think. It's ready and vaiting for us right now."

*What are you doing, man? Bringing her into our life this way?*

Maybe he was trying too hard to be a hero, o live up to his father's reputation. Yeah. Had o be that. He couldn't let it be anything more.

"You live with your grandma and sister?"

"In an apartment over the garage. I like to stay lose. Be the man of the family, if they ever need toilet unclogged or a sink fixed. That sort of hing. Not that my sister couldn't do that, mind ou, but why not ask me to do it instead? What

else am I good for?" He sent her a grin, hoping
to disarm her.

Cade drove back through Mountain Cove
proper where the snow had all but stopped. Rain
was forecasted at the lower elevations later this
week, which would make things a slushy mess.
He waited to see if Leah would ask him again
about a motel, but she stayed silent. Apparently she was accepting his invitation. Finally
he turned onto the road that led to Huckleberry
Hill, a subdivision above the snow line that overlooked Mountain Cove. A few hundred yards up
and the snow started in full force again.

"Got any other family?"

He liked that she was engaging him in conversation. "Sure. My older brother, David, is a
firefighter here in Mountain Cove, has his own
place. He was at the rescue today but I doubt you
met him. I have two younger siblings. Heidi, who
you'll meet at my grandmother's tonight, and
Adam, who has his own apartment. They both
work at the avalanche center with me. We're all
search and rescue volunteers." Following in their
father's footsteps.

Cade turned into the steep driveway, steering through the twists and turns until he was
in front of the two-story home. He parked his
truck and looked at Leah. "What do you say?
Are you hungry?"

If he could get her to eat, he could get her to stay. For tonight, at least, and then he'd sleep better knowing she was, for the time being, out of harm's way. But the way she kept looking at the mirror, watching as if someone might follow, he doubted she'd feel safe no matter where she stayed.

# SIX

"I don't know." She weighed her options. Di[d]
she have any?

She never wanted to face Snyder alone again.
Not on a mountain. Not in that cabin. Not in [a]
motel she might pick to stay the night befor[e]
fleeing again. She hadn't been able to escap[e]
the gripping terror brought on by the sound o[f]
his voice resounding in the cabin. His threat[s]
echoed through her mind, and her only relie[f]
had been Cade's reassuring voice as he tried t[o]
make conversation.

He'd rescued her again. Did he know? Sh[e]
wished she could thank him for that.

She eyed the thick snow that had started u[p]
again, swirling beneath the security light nea[r]
the street, reminding her of the nasty storm. Sh[e]
wished she hadn't asked him about his family[.]
This was getting too personal.

Cade turned off the ignition as though she'[d]

already given an answer. Confident guy. But in his case, he had a reason to be—after all, she'd let him drive her all the way up here.

Leah had been on her own for a long time. Could take care of herself. But right now, the last thing she wanted was to face a cold, dark night alone. The images he'd painted of beef stew, homemade rolls and a cozy home with family waiting ignited the hunger pangs inside of her for more than just food. Sitting in the cab of Cade's warm truck, in his presence, raised her awareness in other ways, too.

She'd always felt confident and secure in her independence. The world she'd built for herself. Didn't want to depend on anyone. Yet she was starving with a need for exactly that. To trust. The need to feel safe and secure. She hadn't known the need was even there inside her, but then, she'd never witnessed a murder before. Never been hunted by an angry predator before.

Staying in the remote cabin hadn't worked. Out of the way as it was, it hadn't been off-grid enough.

"Leah," Cade said, "you have to eat. I know you're hungry. What's holding you back? Am I such a terrible guy?"

Why did he care what she did or what she thought of him? That's what she didn't get. She read the questions behind his intense green gaze—but also saw the protector in him. And maybe that was driving him. "Still doing your job?"

"All part of a day's work." That grin she liked came out again.

"Well, then, thank you. Beef stew sounds wonderful." She opened the door, the cold nearly slapping sense into her, but not quite.

She'd eat and then decide whether or not she'd stay for the night in his grandmother's house. Of course, that also depended on Cade and his family—if the invitation he'd offered on his grandmother's behalf still stood once the woman actually met her.

He escorted her to the front door of the light gray home and ushered her inside. The aroma of fresh-baked bread and beef stew—as promised—wafted around her along with something else she hadn't felt in a long time. If ever.

Love. It was palpable.

Hanging on the wall was a lovely framed cross-stitch that read, "Do not withhold good from those who deserve it, when it is in your power to act. Proverbs 3:27."

Yeah. Leah could see that in Cade. It was part of his upbringing.

The cozy atmosphere and inviting smells almost overwhelmed her. She and Cade took off their coats and dusted off the snow, leaving pudlles on the floor. It was then that she noticed he carried a concealed weapon in a shoulder holster beneath his coat.

She felt her eyes grow wide as her gaze lingered on the weapon. She looked from the gun to Cade's face.

Noticing her surprise, he frowned and disarmed himself. Not that he owed her an explanation, but she wanted one all the same.

She never got one.

Two women entered the foyer that opened into a living room. One was obviously Cade's grandmother, her silver roots battling bushy auburn hair. The other woman—was that his sister? With big brown eyes, she looked nothing like him, except that she shared the same thick, coffee-brown hair.

"Glad you finally made it." The younger woman stepped forward and smiled.

Oh, wait. She had Cade's smile. A nice smile.

"This is Leah Marks," Cade said by way of introduction. "Leah, Heidi, my sister, and this is my grandmother. We call her Grandma Katy or just plain Grandma." He chuckled.

At Leah's name, recognition flashed in Heidi's eyes.

"Nice to meet you," Leah said.

She hoped they wouldn't ask too many questions. Maybe coming here had been a mistake.

She was too exhausted to keep her guard up.
Why hadn't she thought this through? "I hope
I'm not intruding. Your brother invited me."

Cade's grandmother reached over and took
Leah's hand. "Of course you're not intruding,
dear. We're so pleased to have you. And you can
call me Katy."

"Okay, Katy. Thanks," Leah said.

"This is a first," Katy said.

"A first?"

"Cade has never invited a rescue victim over
for dinner before," Heidi said.

Oh.

Katy escorted Leah into the dining room
where dinner plates were set out as though it
was still only six in the evening instead of nearly
eight o'clock. Cade had mentioned his grandmother kept the food warm for him, and some
people ate that late anyway. She would die of
hunger if she waited that late to eat, and that
was probably why Cade had so easily talked her
into this.

"Have a seat, Leah," Katy said. "I'll bring in
the stew and heat up the rolls."

"Thank you." Leah slid into a seat at the dining table, feeling more awkward by the minute.

"I'll be right back." Cade disappeared.

Leah was left sitting alone in the dining room.
She stared out the large window that was meant

to take advantage of the incredible view during the day, but at night only darkness stared back. Leah stood and went to the window, hoping to see past her own reflection. Was Snyder out there now, watching her? She fingered the thick curtains, wondering if Katy would mind if she closed the miniblinds. If Katy knew the kind of person that might be out there, she most certainly wouldn't mind. Leah closed the blinds and peeked through. Someone touched her shoulder from behind. Leah jumped.

"I didn't mean to startle you," Cade said.

"No problem." Leah moved back to her seat, aware that Cade was watching. Funny that he hadn't asked her why she'd closed the blinds.

He probably knew she was exhausted. Vulnerable. Maybe he even knew she was terrified. And he'd brought her to his home so he could feed her well. She almost smiled at the thought. Things could have gone much differently.

Regardless of his thoughtfulness, she couldn't let herself be used and abused the way her mother had been. She would only trust Cade to a point, and never with the truth. Never with even a small part of her heart.

Just as Cade's grandmother set the stew on the table, a yawn overtook Leah. Katy ladled a big helping into Leah's bowl. Then Cade's. He said grace and thanked the Lord for Leah's survival today. Leah could swear she heard tears in his voice as he thanked his Heavenly Father for allowing him to save someone from the claws of an avalanche.

She heard the pain and knew it went deep. That couldn't be for her. There had to be much more to the story and she figured it had to do with his father. She yawned again before he ever said amen. Considering the events of the day and the fact that since witnessing Tim's murder she hadn't been able to sleep, it made sense that exhaustion would catch up to her.

Her cheeks warmed. "I'm so sorry."

Katy patted her shoulder. "You'd better eat up before you fall over. Cade informed me you need a place to stay tonight. We have several extra rooms and there's one all ready for you."

Leah took in a breath to argue; she hadn't told him she was staying yet. Not wanting to endanger someone because of her predicament, she throttled him with her gaze for his presumption. But she couldn't blame him. He didn't know what she was up against. Who he'd brought into this house.

She'd find somewhere else to stay, somewhere safe.

Her mind scrambled to process this life he lived like something from the fifties. A loving grandmother to cook and keep meals warm for him in a nice, cozy home. A protective sister, too, and brothers. A family.

Or was this normal? Leah really couldn't say. She'd never had a real father. Only her mother's various abusive boyfriends. She could only watch other families from the outside.

Unable to disappoint his sweet grandmother, Leah knew that rejecting her offer wasn't the right thing to do. She couldn't hurt Katy's feelings by refusing to accept her kindness. And after what Cade had done for her today, after listening to his heartfelt prayer of thanks, she knew she had to stay the night. At least this one night.

She couldn't think of a safer place than right here where Cade Warren made it his business to watch over things like a sentinel.

With the decision made, relief washed through her, even though she hadn't exactly made the decision herself. But she was a free agent—could walk out at any moment. Stew and bread before her... A warm bed waiting for her upstairs... Safety. Security. For now.

Besides, she couldn't walk out when she was this exhausted. She wasn't free, after all.

"Thank you, really," Leah said. "I don't want to be any trouble."

"No trouble at all, dear."

But Katy couldn't know how far from the truth her words were.

* * *

Cade shared the details of the rescue with Grandma and Heidi while he ate. Leah kept quiet through most of it, not adding to his story. Not shedding any light on why she'd been on the mountain. Never mentioning who the witness was or the other victim.

Right now she was busy eating Grandma's stew. Cade was glad to see she had a hearty appetite after the day she'd had. He knew his grandmother would take care of Leah, as much or as little as she would allow. When Grandma had moved in with them, she had thrived as she'd looked after him, his siblings and his father before he'd died, making this house into a home again.

He chafed at the reminder he'd lost both his parents. But he had his siblings.

Heidi busied herself between the kitchen and the dining room, cleaning up and putting away dishes and hovering near the table. She'd been filing reports today at the avalanche center and not on call; otherwise she would have been involved in the search and rescue, as well.

When Leah attempted to hide another yawn, Grandma stood. "Leah, I'm happy to show you the bedroom where you can sleep if you're ready."

Leah smiled at Grandma, much of the tension

and fear he'd seen in her face today, even moments before when she peered out the window, fading away.

"Yes, thank you," she said.

She grabbed her glass, dish and utensils, and made for the sink, but Heidi quickly whisked them from her. "I'll take those."

Cade was surprised that Leah didn't put up more of a fight, insisting on doing her part, but she looked ready to collapse. Exhaustion weighed on him, as well.

Before she followed Grandma, she glanced in Cade's direction, the gratitude in her gaze meaning more than words ever could. He'd been right to bring her here, at least for tonight.

Cade stood, took his dishes to the sink and chuckled that Heidi didn't whisk his away, too. But, hey, this was an equal opportunity home and it wasn't as if he was a guest. He had as much right to wash a dish as the women. He rinsed his dish and stuck it in the dishwasher, then opened the fridge looking for something with fizz, aware of Heidi's gaze boring into the back of his head.

"What?" he asked. But knowing full well why she stared.

"What's going on?" At the sink, she worked on the rest of the dishes. "What's with bringing an avalanche survivor home?"

He turned around, popping the top on the can of soda he'd grabbed. "Is there a problem with that?"

She shook her head. "No, of course not. It's just not usually done. At least not something *you* usually do. You must have a reason."

"I'm not sure." Cade scratched his neck. "She seemed lost and dazed. She needed a place to stay."

Heidi crossed her arms. Tilted her head. Cocked a brow. "Really?"

"Yes, really. What do you think?"

"I think you're a softie. And here I thought you always threw those walls up, keeping your distance. But this one...she's pretty."

"Don't even go there," Cade growled. He leaned on the kitchen counter and weighed his decision to bring Leah home. He didn't think he'd really had a choice, but getting into all that with his sister wasn't something he was prepared to do yet. That was the problem with living in proximity to his family. Good thing he could escape to his apartment above the garage.

"Where's she from?" Heidi would persist until she had answers. "What was she doing on the mountain?"

"Don't know anything except she was living in old Devon Hemphill's cabin."

Heidi sucked in a breath. Cade wished he hadn't said that much.

The front door opened and shut. "Anybody home?"

They heard rustling sounds for a few seconds—someone slipping out of their winter wear—then David found them in the kitchen, his eyes scanning the counter and table. "You didn't leave me any food?"

Heidi popped him with a towel. "You don't live here. And you don't eat here. You wanted your cool bachelor pad, remember?" She batted her eyelashes. "But I could warm something up for you."

David shook his head at her antics. "Nah, I'm good. Grabbed a bite with the boys. Was just teasing you." He removed his wet cap and raked a hand through his disheveled hair.

"What have you got?" Cade asked.

"Nothing. You already know we ended the search. With this storm coming in, we might not recover the victim until spring thaw."

Cade's gut twisted.

"The only thing we found was a knife," David said. "The good news is you were there in time to dig someone out alive."

Heidi gestured above them. "Not only did he dig her out, he brought her home."

David's eyes widened. "What? Why?"

"Why not?" Cade shoved from the counter
done with this conversation. He couldn't give
them answers he didn't have. He didn't want his
siblings getting too nosy, either. Spooking Leah
He didn't feel comfortable sharing that he believed something was very wrong. It could all
be his imagination. He wished that was the case
but he didn't think so.

David and Heidi followed him into the living
room. A step creaked. They all turned to see
Grandma.

"Leah is tucked away now." She said it as
though Leah were a small child. "I'm heading
to bed myself. Oh, David…" She hurried the rest
of the way down the stairs to give him a peck
on the cheek. "I haven't seen you in ages. Why
didn't you tell us you would stop by? We could
have kept dinner warm."

Cade took that as an opportunity to leave
"'Night, Grandma. I'm heading up to my apartment." He leaned in to give her a quick hug and a
kiss on the cheek. "The stew was your best yet."

He exited through the back door and headed
up the steps to his over-the-garage living space
Once inside, he flipped on the lights and let the
adrenaline drain from his body, though tension
still coiled around his shoulders. Scared and possibly in trouble, Leah Marks was sleeping under
his family's roof. Tomorrow, Cade would try to

onvince her to stay here until the storm passed nd then he'd help her dig the cabin out. She'd aid a friend was letting her stay there, but she adn't said for how long. Still, Cade could check o see what repairs needed to be done, if any. If he was going to stay for any length of time, the lace likely needed some work.

Yeah, and he was the guy to do it, too. Right. Vhy did he think she would even agree? Or that he needed or wanted his help? Leah could work t Home Depot, or be a handyman herself, for all e knew. But the churning in his gut kept him etermined to make sure she was okay.

Cade didn't like to think that he had any lterior motives for wanting to help. Never mind hat it was Devon's cabin—and if Cade made a ew repairs, he could get inside and look around or answers. Some clue to the feud between )evon and Cade's father. Never mind that Cade ad had an entire year to do that while the cabin vas unoccupied. Who would know or care if he'd one to look inside? Except he didn't have a key nd getting inside without a key or permission vould be breaking and entering.

Not the actions of a hero. Not something his ather would have done. But it would be worth if it got him answers. Cade wanted to know vhy his father had died that day. It shouldn't have appened. It didn't make sense.

He'd shared the story with Leah, hoping tha
she would confess what she was doing staying i
the cabin. What or who she was hiding from. Bu
that had apparently been asking too much. H
thought back to the moment when he'd knocke
on the cabin door and it had flown open, Lea
rushing out and into his arms.

The fear and panic in her eyes had nearly don
him in. Maybe she'd simply been afraid of stay
ing in a lonely cabin in the middle of a storm
Alaska night, especially after what she'd bee
through. Who wouldn't be?

Cade was reading too much into this whol
situation. Had to be. But whether she was trul
in danger or not, the real question he had to as
himself was, why did he care so much?

He couldn't lie to himself. The moment he'
pulled her from what could have been her grav
in the snow, the instant he'd looked into he
crystal blue-greens, he'd connected with he
formed some sort of emotional attachment. H
should have walked away as he always did afte
a search and rescue. After he'd completed hi
SAR responsibilities, retrieved the lost or injure
party—whether dead or alive—Cade Warren al
ways walked away.

Never looked back.

What was wrong with him this time? Why ha
he gotten so attached, particularly to a woma

who seemed unwilling to let him in? She was hiding things from him, which should have been warning enough to keep his distance. He'd been through that already. He couldn't let himself grow close, couldn't let this connection or whatever it was between him and Leah go any further. He'd never forgotten how it had felt catching Melissa with another man.

Rising, he moved to the window to twist the blinds closed, the thought reminding him of when Leah had done the same in the dining room earlier that evening. Looking outside, he saw that the snow had diminished to barely visible pinpricks. He let his gaze sweep over the snowdrifts between the trees and down the twisted driveway to the lights of Mountain Cove below the hill.

Thirty yards out something moved in the shadows beneath the trees.

Cade peered closer, stunned at what he saw.

A man dressed in black.

# SEVEN

The soft bed conformed to her body perfectly
Leah rolled onto her side, the aroma of bacon
wafting over her. She bolted straight up. Where
was she?

Cade's face came to mind, along with Katy'
and Heidi's. She was in their home. Safe. She
breathed a sigh of relief, though she could neve
completely relax. Not with a killer after her.

The digital clock read 8:00 a.m. and only th
faint, gray light of morning peeked through th
blinds.

A Bible lay on the side table. She'd seen it las
night but had been too exhausted to look throug
the pages. Instead she'd fallen asleep praying
God had brought her to this place of safety s
she could at least catch her breath. She wouldn
question that. And He'd put her in a Christia
home. After hearing Cade say the blessing befor
their dinner, she had no doubt his faith went deep

But staying one night didn't mean she shoul

ay longer. She climbed from the bed and dug
r clean clothes in her duffel bag. She'd been
o traumatized, too drained, to figure out what
e would do when morning came. Nor had she
ought beyond getting to the cabin when she'd
rst fled from Snyder—getting to Alaska and
aying alive had been her first priority.

It had been difficult enough to find the place.
he'd spent the first couple of days making sure
e could survive there, stocking up on fuel for
e generator and food in case she got snowed
. She hadn't progressed to investigating Sny-
er, which would have been hard to do anyway
ithout internet at the cabin, not to mention
r away from the city where the crime had oc-
urred. She'd steered clear of civilization because
eing off grid was meant to have kept her safe,
ut it hadn't worked. How had Snyder found her?
ow could she keep him from finding her again?

She couldn't research if she was dead.

Was there wireless internet access here? Leah
ulled out her laptop and set it on the small sec-
tary desk against the wall. She flipped on the
esk lamp. Her laptop booted up. Yes. Of course,
ade and Heidi would have Wi-Fi. Maybe Katy
ven enjoyed the social media sites. Again, Leah
lt the pain of being utterly alone in this world,
ith no family except her aunt in Florida. And

now she didn't even have a job. But those wer
selfish thoughts considering Tim had lost his lif

She focused her attention on her compute
finding a strong wireless signal. The famil
hadn't set things up to require a password, eithe
Her heart raced. Getting research time in coul
mean the difference between life and death. Sh
hoped that connecting to cyberspace would hel
her find the evidence she would need again
Snyder. Somewhere there had to be somethin
that would give her the clues she needed.

And that was all part of Leah's job as a leg
investigator.

She glanced around the quaint room, no
ing more cross-stitched pictures, some of the
Bible verses. This was a well-kept and well-love
home. So opposite of what she'd known growin
up. A person could get used to this. Well, an
person that wasn't her. She couldn't put thes
people in danger.

Chances were good that Snyder had alread
searched the local motels. There weren't th
many in the small town. Eventually he woul
have found her if she'd stayed in one of them. Sh
would have been awake all night worrying abo
that. If the storm hadn't hit, and Snyder hadn
come back to the cabin to find her, she woul
have gotten in her SUV and driven…somewher
Except she couldn't drive her way out of Mou

in Cove. If she wanted to leave, she'd have to take a ferry along the Alaska Marine Highway north to Haines or Skagway, or south to Juneau where she could catch a flight out of southeast Alaska.

The truth is she had no idea where she could go to be safe since this plan hadn't worked. But Snyder had no idea where she was at the moment. How could he know that she was staying with a local family? And which one, at that? Though she couldn't stay here long, she should at least pray about staying long enough to get her bearings.

A scraping noise outside caught her attention.

She went to the window and peeked through the miniblinds, morning light finally brightening the skies. Cade was shoveling snow below her. The sight brought a smile to her lips. She owed it to him to help with that.

But maybe she could help him in a better way...

Tim hadn't even known the cabin existed until a few months ago when he'd found out his distant uncle had died and Tim had inherited the property. It hadn't made sense because Devon had had a daughter. But she'd simply disappeared. Though Tim had made an initial trip to see the cabin, he'd hoped Leah could conduct further investigation regarding the disappear-

ance of his distant cousin. He'd wanted to pas
the cabin over to what he thought of as the right
ful owner. So she really did have a mostly legiti
mate reason to be in the cabin, though she coul
tell Cade hadn't believed her story. Finding ou
more about Devon Hemphill could help Cade
too, if she could dig deep enough to discover th
reason for a family feud that even Cade himsel
couldn't figure out.

Leah shoved all that aside for now and wen
back to the laptop, searching for information on
Detective Nick Snyder. Head in her hands, sh
stared at the laptop. There was the story of Tim'
murder and the ongoing investigation conducted
by none other than Detective Snyder himself
Then another story the week before of Snyder'
role in a sting operation to bring down a drug
ring.

How did the guy do that? It was as though
there were two sides to the man. Hero on the on
side and villain on the other. He hadn't earned
his position by being a lousy detective; he knew
how to sniff out criminals.

So why had he killed Tim? If she could fig
ure that out, then she'd know what Snyder wa
after—and why he was desperate enough to
have to follow her here. He had to know she
hadn't taken a photograph of him because she

would have already exposed his secret identity as a murderer.

She had to figure out what was going on between Tim and Snyder.

Closing her eyes, she thought back to the weeks leading up to Tim's murder. He'd acted strange. Had had a few too many private phone calls…had snapped at her and been irritable when she'd walked into his office… She was his investigator, and he'd never treated her that way, so she'd known something was up. But Tim hadn't been in a sharing frame of mind.

A creature of habit, he'd had protocols in place for everything. Leah knew all of those as had his paralegal, Sheila, who was out on maternity leave. Leah thanked God for that small kindness, otherwise Sheila might have ended up in Snyder's crosshairs, too. Tim hadn't wanted to bring in a temp, so filing was backlogged, which wasn't a good thing for an attorney's office. Letting the office run shorthanded was unlike Tim and she had wondered at it at the time. Now Leah understood—he'd known something bad was coming down and had wanted as many people as possible out of the way. Sheila on maternity leave…Leah on vacation…Tim facing down the oncoming danger alone…

Leah knew Tim's habits well enough that she knew where he put sensitive documents. Except

this time. And he would have known that sh
might be in danger, too, if what Tim had planne
turned south.

Her pulse ratcheted up as the image replaye
across her mind.

Leah had gone back to the office and parke
on the street. She'd spotted Tim from a distanc
in the parking garage when Snyder had showe
up, railing, *"Think I'm going to take this fron
a scumbag like you?"* Snyder had whipped ou
a gun with a sound suppressor and shot Tim i
the head.

Leah had taken her share of incriminatin
photographs in her role as investigator, but neve
of an actual murder in the making. She shoul
have tried to stop him. Something. But it ha
happened too fast. She'd frozen and flattene
her body behind the concrete beam, squeezin
her eyes shut and praying for her life. *Oh, Goo
Oh, God, Oh, God... Let him not find me here.*

Snyder had gotten into his car and driven off
As he'd exited the parking garage, he'd glance
over and seen Leah. It was all over then. Lik
so many of those police chases she'd witnesse
she expected Snyder to chase her down. To tel
the police that she'd shot and killed Tim to cove
for his deed.

But none of that had happened. It was insan
ity. She'd driven to the airport and parked, hop

ıg to mislead him, and then she'd taken a cab
) the ferry that would take her through the In-
ıde Passage to Mountain Cove. To Tim's cabin.

She pressed her palms into her eyes, pushing
ıack the tears, her breaths raspy. "Oh, Tim, what
ıd you get into with that man?"

She replayed Snyder's words in her head. *Take
ıis from a scumbag... Take this from a scum-
ıag... Take this from a scumbag...*

Take what?

Leah thought of all the possibilities.

Someone rapped softly on the door.

"Leah? Breakfast is ready," Katy said through
ıe door.

Leah cracked it. "Thank you. I'll be right
own."

Leah finished dressing, brushed her hair and
ırabbed her toothbrush for a stop at the bath-
ıoom, but right before she left the bedroom, the
ıhoveling stopped outside. She heard voices and
ıeeked out the window again.

Cade was speaking with a police officer, show-
ıg him the gun she'd seen on him last night as
ˉit was a new toy.

Leah jerked back, her pulse jumping to her
ıroat. Normally law enforcement would be a
ıood thing to have around, but the fewer people
ıho knew she was here, the better, especially
ıiven the police channels to which Snyder had

access. With his reputation, he could easily tur
the police force against her. She had a feelin
the only reason she wasn't already a suspect i
Tim's murder was that Snyder needed somethin
from her. And the words he said before she
heard Cade's voice at the cabin door last nigh
flooded back to her.

*"If I don't get what I want then I'm going t
pin Tim's murder on you. I have all the evidenc
I need to do it, and you helped me when you fle
the scene. The next thing I'm going to do is ki
you."*

Of course, Snyder's evidence would be ci
cumstantial or planted. But it would be her wor
against Snyder's—if she was even alive at tha
point to speak in her own defense. If only sh
knew what he was after. Was it evidence again
him—perhaps something Tim had found? Mayb
that's exactly what Tim had been about to do—
use the evidence he had against Snyder—bu
Snyder had killed him before he could do any
thing.

Now Snyder would do the same to Leah. H
had her on the run and scared for her life, whic
was all part of his plan. She understood why Ti
had sent her away now. She'd been suspicious c
her own boss, knowing something was going or
but she'd been too slow in figuring things ou
None of that mattered now.

In the end Snyder would kill her whether or ot he got what he wanted because he couldn't fford to leave the one witness to Tim's murder ive.

Cade glanced at his watch and said goodbye Terry Stratford, a close friend he'd grown up ith who now worked for Mountain Cove PD. ade had told him he thought he'd seen someone utside watching the house last night and he'd ne to investigate. Terry knew Cade would have weapon, something to defend himself with, and en they'd started talking about Cade's new gun, .44 Magnum.

He put the shovel away in the garage and lanced across the yard into the wood that sep- ated this house from the next one. Last night, ith flashlight in hand, he'd seen footprints that nfirmed he hadn't imagined the person he'd en outside. Someone had been watching the use.

This morning those footprints were gone, of urse, after the sky dumped more snow during e night. Funny that the guy had been dressed black like the witness at the avalanche, though at could be simply coincidence. It didn't prove ything. But he didn't believe in coincidences.

Cade stomped his boots to knock the snow off en stepped through the back door. Leah sat at

the kitchen table alone, eating a piece of baco
Her cheeks warmed when she saw him watchin

"Hey. I don't want to track slush through th
house, but I wanted to let you know I'm head
ing back to work at the avalanche center. Was
the office at six this morning already, workin
on the forecast. Heidi's there now. I came bac
to shovel more snow for Grandma so she coul
get out if she needed to."

That brought a half smile to Leah's pretty fac
She should smile more often. Cade wished l
could come all the way inside and sit at the tabl
Drink coffee with her. Get to know her better s
he could help her get settled in safely. Find o
what repairs she needed at the cabin. What sl
might know about someone watching the hou
last night. He struggled with whether or not t
say anything about what he'd seen. If she knev
she might try to leave the safety of his hom
and from what he could tell, she was all alone i
whatever trouble she was in. He wished he kne
what was going on. Guessing all the time wa
driving him crazy, but he was a patient man. H
could wait for her to tell him.

"Your grandmother is on the phone," she sai
"I'll give her the message."

"Listen," Cade said, "we got record snowfa
here last night, so that means even more for th
cabin. I know I said I'd help you put a plow c

our vehicle, but getting back there today is not uch a good idea. Besides, I need to get the right ttachment. When the weather clears up more, I an go with you to take a look at anything that eeds repair in the cabin, too."

"Or fix a sink or unclog a toilet? Except there's o toilet unless you count the outhouse." She gave n exaggerated shudder to which Cade chuckled. 'You're a real handyman, Cade, but I'm used to iving on my own and taking care of myself."

"I'm sure you're completely capable of handling anything," he said. "I'm just offering some elp. Hey, even I have to ask Heidi to hold a vrench once in a while." He hoped she heard he teasing in his tone.

Leah stood from the table and strolled toward im. Arms crossed, she leaned against the couner, a tan turtleneck hugging her slim body. "I aw you talking to a police officer outside. Any nore news about the other victim? Did they find nyone else?"

"No. But my brother said they found a knife n the debris field."

She recoiled. "A knife?"

"That wouldn't have been yours, would it?" He njected the question with a teasing tone.

She shook her head too quickly. "Of course ot."

"That wasn't an accusation." He'd been trying to make a joke, but he'd clearly chosen a touchy subject. Idiot. "Relax. I didn't mean to sound judgmental. People carry knives all the time around here, especially in the wilderness. They carry guns, too."

"Like the one I saw you with last night? The one you were showing the officer this morning."

"Yes, like that one. That's only one of several weapons I own." He cocked a brow. Took a guess. "You're not from Alaska, are you?"

"Uh. No."

Didn't think so. "Alaskans love their guns. In my case, I do a lot of work in the field and I'm always armed in case I run into a brown bear, bigger than grizzlies here in Alaska. And if you stay at the cabin, you should have protection, too. If you'd like I can help you learn how to fire one."

He took a step closer at the risk of letting the muck melt onto Grandma's clean floor.

"I know how to use a gun, Cade. I had one on the mountain with me when I got caught in the avalanche. I was actually hoping the rescuers found it." Her words surprised him, considering her reaction to the knife and to the sight of his holster.

The mystery Leah Marks brought was almost like the cornices loaded with too much snow ready to bury him if he disturbed them.

Once again he wondered if he should tell her

hat someone had been outside the house last ight, watching from the woods. He didn't want o scare her, though he knew she was strong. He aw a fire inside Leah. Determination. He liked hat way more than he should. In the face of that trength, what right did he have to keep the truth rom her? But he knew if he told her about some-ne watching the house, and if she believed it had o do with her, then she would leave.

His throat constricted. He admitted he didn't vant her to go away for a far deeper reason than imply keeping her safe or because he wanted an-wers that he believed he might find in the cabin.

Leah slow-blinked and looked away. "Thank ou for letting me stay last night. For saving my ife. I appreciate everything you've done for me, ut I need to get going as soon as I can—as you ay, when the weather clears. We don't need to o back to the cabin until then. And I won't need epairs in the cabin because I don't plan to stay. need to get my SUV, though."

Wait. What? "I asked you last night if you vere in trouble, Leah. What's going on? I want o help."

When she looked back at him, her blue-greens ocked on his gaze like crampons clawing into he glacier of his heart. He could hardly breathe.

A small laugh escaped, sounding forced. "You ave an overactive imagination. I'm a legal investigator by trade, so believe me, I know how to take care of myself. The situations I can get into are pretty rough sometimes, hence the gun. So you don't need to worry about me, Cade. I'll be leaving the area soon, anyway."

Disappointment surged.

"Then you're heading back to wherever you came from. Where would that be?"

Leah smiled the kind of smile that told him he was asking too many questions. "I need to do some research before I leave Mountain Cove altogether. I was planning to go to a motel…"

The way she let her words trail off—was she asking him what he thought she was asking?

"You're welcome to stay here as long as you need."

What was he doing?

Relief washed over her features. "Are you sure? Because I don't want to take advantage of your generosity. It won't be for long."

"Of course, I'm sure. Grandma and Heidi will love another woman in the house." Cade didn't even want to think about how much he wanted Leah to stay. Or why. He only wanted to help. Uh-huh.

"While I'm here, I thought I could help you in your search for answers."

"Answers?" She was going to help him? He thought *he* was helping *her.*

"About whatever happened between your father and Devon Hemphill. Though come to think of it, if we're looking for insight into that, we might need to go back to the cabin for more than any vehicle."

Cade shifted in his boots, sweating under his collar. He didn't have time to take off his coat. He had to get going. And yet here he was, still trying to make sense of this bewildering woman.

He shrugged. "How could you help me? The quarrel was likely something buried and very personal. Not a legal matter at all." He said the words but still hoped she'd be able to find something.

"You do your job and let me do mine. I'm quite good at it, actually. I know how to find evidence to prove someone's innocence or guilt." Her eyes grew dark. "I know how to find evidence to put killers away."

A chill slithered along Cade's spine. What was that about?

# EIGHT

Three days later Leah felt as if she was getting
cabin fever. At least she wasn't stuck in the real
cabin up the mountain practically living like a
pioneer. Though she was grateful to Cade and
his family for allowing her to stay, for not pry-
ing into her life, Leah grew frustrated that she
hadn't been able to find out more about Snyder.

At least she hadn't been able to spot him in
Mountain Cove. He'd likely had to travel back
to Washington to show his face and do his real
job instead of stalking her. She'd counted on
the fact he couldn't know where she was, but
he was a smart man. Sooner or later he would
figure out she hadn't left Mountain Cove, after
all. She only hoped that by the time he realized
that, she'd have found evidence that she could
use against him.

At least she'd made a few discoveries by accessing the files in Tim's online database. She
had pulled up all the digital files of cases they

had worked on over the past year, looking for something that connected them, starting with their ages and birthdates. Types of crimes. Those whom Tim had gotten off and those few who had ended up going to prison. Tim had been a great defense attorney, making a name for himself. Starting in alphabetical order, she had done an internet search on each of the clients in her files.

Obituaries for at least three of Tim's recent clients had showed up in the search.

Leah logged in again now, so she could cross-reference the client list, find out if she was on to something. Or at least she tried to log in, but her access was denied.

"No." She shoved from the desk and clenched her fists.

Tim would have assigned another attorney to close his office in case of his death. The first thing the new attorney would do is go through files to find out which ones needed immediate action. It would take time to close Tim's practice, and she doubted anything had been moved from his office yet. Clients would be contacted and must then decide on new representation. But apparently the attorney had already changed the password, not even bothering to talk to Leah about anything. But then...she'd made herself pretty unavailable. Maybe he thought her strange for not rushing back from her *cruise* upon learning of Tim's death. He'd likely talked to Sheila if he needed anything.

Looked as though Leah would have to access the physical files. Go back to Tim's office.

A noise downstairs startled her. Once again Leah wished the SAR volunteers had found her gun on the mountain. She'd made a few trips into town but always with Katy, and Leah hadn't felt comfortable buying a gun in her presence. At the sound downstairs, she thought of Cade's gun, wishing she had it in her hands right now. Wishing she had access to the other weapons he had mentioned but hadn't showed her.

She crept down the stairs and found Katy unpacking groceries. She hadn't even realized the woman had left the house. She'd let her guard down too much.

Katy's eyes grew wide. "Leah, I didn't realize you were still here. Cade mentioned wanting to take you back to the cabin now that the streets are clear. He's working at the center today instead of doing field work. I always worry about him and Adam or Isaiah, whoever goes with him. But I thought he'd already come by to get you."

Funny, Cade hadn't mentioned that to her, but he'd left the house before she'd gotten up. "No, yet. But don't worry, I'll be out of here soon enough."

"No rush, dear. None at all. You stay as long

as you need. But we get things done while the weather allows. I expect it'll start raining. It snows one week, then rains the next."

So she'd be smart to get her vehicle while the weather cooperated. Once she had her ride back she would be free to leave this sweet family. But she wished she had something to give Cade in return before she left. She hadn't had much success in tracking down Devon's daughter—another missing piece of the Warren family feud puzzle. The daughter might be able to answer a few questions. One thing she suspected—the cabin itself didn't hold any answers for Cade as he hoped. No. If there were answers to find, they were probably in the box full of papers and letters that Tim had brought back with him from his one trip to the cabin after inheriting it.

Leah helped Katy unpack the groceries. What had Cade told his grandmother about Leah and why she needed to stay here? If anything, Leah was like a stray they'd taken in, and she hoped to remedy that soon enough.

"Oh, I can't believe it." The woman looked through the cabinets. "I thought I had pasta sauce. I hate it when that happens."

She shook her head and poured coffee from a carafe, then moved to a chair at the table. "Getting old isn't for the weak at heart," Katy said with a wink.

Leah chuckled. "I'm happy to go back into town for you and get the pasta sauce. Only, I don't have a vehicle."

And if she was on her own, she could buy a gun while she was in town. It would have to be a rifle or shotgun since she was from out of state, but it would be better than nothing.

Katy eyed Leah over the rim of her cup. "I wouldn't want you to go to any trouble, and Cade will be here at some point. I'll call and ask him to pick some up on the way."

"No, please." Leah tried to sound calm, but she realized how much she wanted some time away from the house. "There are a few items I'd like to get for myself while I'm there. I'll be back before you know it, and Cade can wait for me if he beats me home." She smiled, hoping Katy would agree.

She set her coffee on the table. "If you're sure, then. The keys are right there next to my purse, dear."

"Thank you." Leah took the keys. "Any particular kind of sauce?"

"Ragu. Two large jars of Ragu garlic and onions."

"I'll be back in a few."

With her hands on the steering wheel of Katy's sedan, Leah sucked in a breath, taking control of the unexpected sense of freedom that rushed over her. This wasn't her car, she reminded herself. She couldn't leave town in it. Besides, she had nowhere to go.

She steered carefully down the steep, curvy drive—surprised the homes were spaced this far apart—and through the small subdivision on the hill down into Mountain Cove. She relished the sense of safety that came from the fact that Snyder didn't know where she was this time, and he was likely back at his job until he could break free to track her again. That bought her some time.

But how much? A week? A day? Two hours?

She drove through town along the main thoroughfare until she found the first grocery store. She grabbed two jars of pasta sauce, then headed to the express line behind two others. The temperature was in the high forties today so Leah hadn't worn her parka but dressed in layers instead. She hoped the line would hurry because she didn't want to have to peel out of her layers just to put them back on again. Plus, the quicker she was done here, the more time she'd have to look into getting a weapon.

Pasta sauce bagged and in hand, Leah headed out the doors and into the parking lot. She was reaching for the car keys when someone bumped her shoulder, causing her to drop her grocery bag. Startled, Leah whirled around, but the man apologized and kept going. Nothing to be alarmed about. She reached down to grab her sack but didn't see the keys. Where had they gone? When she stood, she glanced across the street.

And locked eyes with Snyder, his face half-hidden behind the hood of his gray-fleeced hoodie.

Terror crushed her lungs, cemented her feet onto the sidewalk. She stood frozen as if time had slowed, and watched Snyder cross the street, moving toward her as though he expected her to stand there and wait.

Um. No. Leah shook off the chains of fear and searched for the keys to the car. She couldn't find them. Would he really come after her in broad daylight in front of all these people? She wouldn't put it past him. But no way would he want to call attention to himself. He would try to keep things low-key. She was counting on that.

Worst case, he could pretend to arrest her, cuff her and take her away. He could easily plant something incriminating on her. Or he could frame her for Tim's murder as he'd said. Her imagination ran away with all the possibilities.

But he would do none of that until he got what he needed from her.

What was it?

No time to think about that now. She glimpsed him push into a jog as he realized she was going to flee from him yet again. Leah got her feet moving and kicked the car keys. She scrambled to pick them up, but it was too late to drive away. Leah took off behind the building. She rushed through an exit door of the appliance store next door right as a worker came out, but unfortunately he called attention to her. She shoved him out and locked the door. No one was around to see so she strode through the employees-only section as though she belonged there, looking for an exit. Leah hurried out the front of the store and jogged down the sidewalk between alleys. If Snyder wanted to keep his apprehension of her low-key, he'd already made one mistake. People had seen him chasing her.

She didn't have time to contemplate all that could mean.

Breathing hard, she ran a good distance and then blended into the early afternoon crowd at the shopping center, finally slipping into a women's undergarment store. She pretended to shop for bras while she gathered her thoughts.

How did she get out of this? How did she escape this nightmare when she didn't have time to breathe, much less figure things out to save her neck?

Before Katy had come home, Leah had been researching Tim's deceased clients with the files she'd been able to access before getting locked out. The week before he'd left to check on the cabin, a client's ex-wife had come to see Tim regarding her ex-husband's death.

That was when Tim had scolded Leah for not taking her vacation time and become adamant that she take a few weeks off. Could it be related?

She glanced out the glass front of the store, watching for Snyder. Holding the keys in her hands, she knew she'd have to make it back to Katy's car. She could only hope Snyder didn't know which car that was, or he might sabotage it. She would get in and drive away and hopefully lose him before he figured out where she was staying.

Leah slipped outside; the clear skies a break in the gray, wintry, wet weather of the region. Birds chirped and flitted, cars filled the parking places along Main Street, the downtown bustled with people going about their business as though nothing at all was wrong.

Reversing her hoodie, she stepped in to the dance, joining the rhythm. She stared at the un-traceable track phone she'd purchased when she'd first arrived in Mountain Cove and walked next to two teenagers, chatting with them as though she knew them. Admiring their boots had brought on smiles and conversation instead of the weird looks she might have invited. But could she do this all the way to back to the grocery store? She didn't know.

The girls moved across the street and Leah's gaze darted to her next target—someone to make it look as if she was with them. Walking alone, she was a far easier target to spot.

A hand twisted her arm and she cried out, tried to move away.

"Scream and I'll kill you here and now," Snyder whispered. "Keep walking."

Her legs were jelly, but she did her best. How had she missed him?

*Oh, God, help me...*

Snyder smiled and nodded to a couple that walked by. He pinched tighter, walking closer to her, making them look like a couple themselves. Her stomach roiled with nausea. She was weak, so weak. She only thought she was strong, but she'd lied to herself.

And then, to Leah's surprise, he yanked her into an alley, into the shadows. He held her from behind, his arm around her throat, his hot breath in her ear.

A decorated town hero. How could he do this?

"This isn't who or what I want to be, Leah, but your boss left me no choice. Here's what's going to happen. I'm going to hurt that family you're staying with if you don't give me what I want. You should never have involved them."

Leah had to be strong and think on her feet in her line of work, but never had she been in this situation. She called upon all the strength she could muster. "You wouldn't *dare* touch them," she snapped. "The more people you mess with the dirtier your hands get and the greater your chances of going down. So. Stay. Away. From Them."

His grip tightened. "Then give me what want."

She struggled to breathe, to speak. "But… don't…know…what…you…want." She could barely creak the words out.

"Don't lie to me!" His hiss revealed his own panic.

And in that moment Leah found strength in his weakness. She threw her head back into his nose, stomped on his foot and turned to kick him in the crotch.

She burst from the alley and crossed the street.

A honk blared in her ears.

A snowplow filled her vision.

Cade slammed on the brakes, his vehicle skidding on the wet street.

And Leah went down.

He tore open the door, fear and panic strangling him as he made it to the front of his truck.

There. She was on the ground, unconscious.

"Someone call 9-1-1!"

A crowd gathered. Concern over Leah along with questions about what had happened swirled around him. He bent over her, checking her vitals, thankful that her pulse was strong.

Sirens blared in the distance.

How had this happened? How had he managed to hit this woman when he'd been on his way to pick her up? "She…came out of nowhere," he whispered to himself. He couldn't believe that he'd rescued her earlier in the week only to take her out today. But had he actually hit her? He didn't think so.

Her eyes fluttered open and those blue-green irises dilated, focusing on him.

*Déjà vu.*

Her face contorted into an expression of fear as she scanned the crowd and tried to get up.

"Easy now," he said, holding her in place. "You're hurt. You shouldn't move. The ambulance will be here soon."

"No!" Her eyes were wide. "No…" Softer this time. "Please, help me up."

He couldn't resist her pleading eyes but the timing worked for him as the gurney rolled up with the EMTs. Cade moved away.

"No, Cade, stay with me," she said.

At this moment the confident legal investigator was nowhere to be found—there was just a scared woman looking to him for help. He moved to her side again and held her hand as the medics gently helped her onto the gurney.

"I'm not going to the hospital," she protested "I'm fine."

Cade frowned and shared a look with Johnny. one of the EMTs he knew well. "I don't know what you have against hospitals, but at least let these guys check you out, okay?" If there was something serious wrong, they could insist on a hospital visit. But Leah had a strong opinion of her own. That much was sure.

She nodded and they wheeled her out of the street and over to the ambulance parked at the side of the road. Cade moved his vehicle over, too, and told Terry Stratford, the police officer on duty, what had happened from his point of view.

Another witness had already explained that Cade had stopped in time but Leah had either slipped or passed out, they weren't sure. She'd hit her head on the street, accounting for the knot. When he explained that Leah was the girl he'd pulled from the avalanche debris days earlier, and that she was also staying in his grandmother's house, Terry chuckled and gave him a hard time.

"Maybe you'd better ask her to marry you before you run into her again and something worse happens," his friend teased.

"It's not like that between us."

"Oh, no? The way you talk about her, could have fooled me."

"I haven't said anything."

"No. More like the way your eyes light up."

Cade glared.

"You could do worse," Terry said, then went back to his cruiser.

Yeah, but Cade knew nothing about her except his suspicions that she was in trouble. What would his police officer friend say if he told him that? Part of Cade wanted to, but not before he found out more himself. Besides, it might be nothing at all, and then Terry would really have a reason to harass him.

No. This was definitely something. Cade hadn't missed the terror on Leah's face as she'd run across the street without even looking. She wasn't going to talk her way out of this one. Cade wouldn't let her this time.

He scraped both of his still-shaking hands through his hair and crushed his eyes shut. He released his pent-up breath, creating a puffy cloud. Man, that had been close. He could have killed her. Once he found his composure, he headed toward the gurney now stuck halfway into the ambulance, and bumped into a sturdy man striding the opposite direction.

Cade glanced back at the man—caught his

dark eyes and grim features tucked beneath the hood of his gray hoodie—and tossed out his apology, then kept walking. There was something familiar about the stranger's face, but he didn't have time to worry about it. He headed to where Johnny stood trying to convince Leah that she needed the hospital.

"It's a small bump on the head," Leah said and climbed off the gurney.

Johnny saw Cade and shrugged.

When Johnny and his coworker had packed up their equipment and were out of earshot, Cade leaned in. "What happened back there? A witness said I didn't hit you, that you collapsed. Either way, you need to see the doc. Maybe this is something residual from being buried in the ice. You sure you don't need a hospital?"

Lights still flashed around them, but the crowd of people had moved on, although some rubber neckers still slowed traffic on Main Street. Leah rubbed her arms and blinked up at him.

"Can you take me home, er, to your house?"

"That's where I was headed when we had our collision," he said. "What were you doing? I had planned to take you to the cabin today." He gently ushered her over to his truck.

They climbed inside and shut the doors before Leah spoke.

"I went to the grocery store for your grand

mother. Her car is still sitting in the parking lot."
Leah frantically searched for something. "Where
are the keys? And the Ragu?"

Cade started his truck. "Relax, I'll see if I can
find the keys, but my grandmother has more than
one set, and we can buy more pasta sauce. You
wait in the truck and stay warm."

Cade was almost afraid to let her out of his
sight. He held his hands up for cars to stop while
he jogged to the middle of the road, lifted the
keys, surprised that no one had picked them up.
He nodded his thanks for the drivers who had
slowed for him, waved goodbye to Johnny as the
ambulance pulled away and headed back to his
truck. The day had warmed up and the snow was
turning to slush.

He glanced up at the clouds. Rain was pre-
dicted this afternoon, at least in the lower
elevations. Up at Leah's—er, Devon Hemphill's—cabin, would be a different story.

Was that guy ogling his truck?

Cade stiffened. He glanced into the cab.

Leah was gone.

# NINE

Leah tried not to panic as she hunkered down o the floorboard of Cade's truck. She was a leg investigator for crying out loud—how had sl been reduced to slinking and hiding like son kind of criminal?

Of course she knew how—Snyder could mak her a criminal, with the full support of a city th adored him. But somewhere…someone else ha to know what was going on. Who Snyder reall was. If only she could get the chance to fin some evidence that proved it. But Tim had fig ured things out and he hadn't even been able t use what he found.

Leah was in over her head. Why didn't sl admit it? Steadying her breaths, she prayed th. God would help her bring Snyder to justic That's all she ever wanted, to help defend th innocent, the falsely accused. She never dreame she would be in this situation.

The driver's side door flew open and Leah's heart jumped into her throat.

Cade slipped inside. He started the vehicle as though she wasn't even there, glancing in the rearview mirror. "You want to tell me what you're doing?"

"I'm, um, I'm hiding. What does it look like?"

Leah hated that she'd involved his family in this. Hated that Snyder had threatened to hurt them, but was determined that she'd be long gone before he would get the chance. Besides— if he was the smart guy she knew he must be, he wouldn't want any more collateral damage than he'd already created with Tim's murder.

Cade steered his truck down the street. "That much is obvious. What sort of trouble are you in?"

Leah slowly climbed back into the seat and buckled herself in. "It's not what you think, Cade, I promise."

There was nothing she wanted more than for this man to think good things about her. But why did it matter? She'd never cared about what others thought before. That would make her too weak—like her mother who gave up everything to please people.

To please men.

Pain burning behind her eyes, Leah turned

her face away from Cade and watched the quai
town coated in white icing pass by.

"You don't know what I think. And you car
know if you don't tell me what is going on. Ho
many times do I have to ask you? Please let n
help."

Cade thought he could fix the world. Or
least rescue it one victim at a time.

"I don't need some hero coming in to save tl
day. I've made it this far without anyone's help
Ouch. She sounded brutal. "I'm sorry. I kno
that's not completely true. I would have died c
the mountain without your help." And mayl
she'd already be dead if she hadn't had the re
uge of Cade's home.

He and his family had extended kindness
her, and how had she repaid them? She'd enda
gered them all because she was weak and neec
and let herself slip. Let herself depend on Cac
a little. Never again. She wished she could te
him everything, but she shoved the thought awa
Trusting someone that much, especially someo
like Cade, could be dangerous to her life pla
To her heart. She wouldn't do it.

"And that night at the cabin…" he said. "We
you running from someone then?"

Telling him anything could end up enda
gering his life. But then again, it was probab
already too late, considering Snyder's threa

Ignoring his question, she said, "I need to get out of town. To leave again. Please take me to your grandmother's car so I can follow you back. Then I'll grab my gear and if you give me a lift to the cabin so I can get my SUV, I'll get out."

She hated to run again before she'd found out what she needed to nail Snyder before he nailed her. But getting out of town was the only way to protect herself—and Cade's family.

"No. You don't have to leave," Cade said. "You don't think I knew something was wrong when I invited you to stay? You looked like someone who needed help." He pulled into the grocery store parking lot and idled next to Katy's car. "I can help you figure this out if you'll let me, Leah. If you're in danger, we can get help."

She pinned him with her gaze. "Why, Cade? Why would you do that?"

He scratched his jaw, appearing to search for an answer that would make sense to both of them. "I've never gone beyond the initial rescue with a victim. Not like this. Not until you. It's almost as if in that moment I pulled you from the snow, I just…couldn't let go." He chuckled softly. "Sounds kind of creepy when said like that. I want to help. It's what I do."

She frowned, staring down at her hands—she'd never seen such complete transparency in another human being and it almost physically hurt. Finally, she gathered enough strength to look back at him, to face him and the question brewing behind his eyes. He'd never been any thing but open and honest with her, and she wa nothing but a liar who'd brought danger to him She'd never needed another person. Not until thi moment—and it was near impossible to rejec his offer.

Reject him.

She placed her hand over his on the console and felt the strength there. Tried to absorb som of his goodness. Telling him everything—well no, that would put him in more danger. "That' sweet of you, Cade. Very sweet."

He frowned. "I wasn't going for sweet."

"You were going for gallant, I know." She chuckled and clasped the door handle. "We'c better get the pasta sauce and head back. You grandmother is going to wonder what happened."

"Oh, she knows. She always knows."

Cade got out with Leah and they made the quick purchase. Back at the vehicles, she climbec inside Katy's car and started it, looking up a him.

"You know your way?" he asked.

She nodded. "I think so, yes."

"Good. I'll follow you there."

Leah exited the parking lot and drove out o town and up the hill, the snowplow grille o

Cade's truck in her rearview mirror serving as a reminder of her near-collision today. Feeling safe and secure had never been on her radar until now, when she was in Cade's presence. That man was the embodiment of safety and security and so much more. She was drawn to him for reasons that mattered, and reasons she couldn't entertain. But her mind was traitorous and her thoughts drifted to what it would feel like to have his strong, protective arms around her. To never live in fear again.

To be loved and cherished.

She shoved the crazy thoughts away. She couldn't afford to think that way, to let her edge slip. Instead she focused on her dire circumstances. It was clear that she wouldn't have any chance to escape if she didn't figure out what Snyder wanted and why he was so desperate. Why had he killed Tim?

Could she trust in Cade's words and let him help? The bigger question was could she trust him once he knew the scope of what she was involved in? It was too dangerous to share with another person, and yet, too dangerous to keep to herself. What did she do? What if something happened to her and the truth never came out? Telling one other person would remedy that—but if Snyder found out that Cade or his family knew, then what would happen to them? On the other

hand, Snyder might think she had already tol[
Cade. If that was the case, he needed to knov
what he was up against.

*God, show me what to do.*

On the short drive out of town and up the hil[
to the house, Cade watched the other cars t[
see if someone followed them. That man in th[
hoodie who had been looking at his truck—wa[
he the same man Cade had seen watching out
side the house? Or was Cade being completel[
paranoid?

Regardless, Cade hated that he'd brought trou[
ble home to his grandmother and sister, but he'[
never been one to turn his back if he could help
If Leah had some crazy ex-boyfriend chasing
her down so he could abuse her, he'd have t[
go through Cade first. If there was one thing h[
couldn't stand it was abusers. And he'd be just a
guilty if he stood on the sidelines and watche[
when he could do something about it.

His father had held to that. And Grandma ha[
that scripture she'd cross-stitched and hung o[
the wall: "Do not withhold good from those wh[
deserve it, when it is in your power to act." Cad[
saw it every day on his way out the front doo[
after breakfast.

He didn't believe he was in the position t[
judge who deserved help and who didn't. Whe[

 he saw Terry again, he would ask him about cruising by the house once in a while to scare the creepers away.

When they arrived at the house, he followed Leah inside to hand off the pasta sauce. Cade had called Grandma to let her know they were on their way.

"Finally." Grandma took the jars. "I'll start the pasta and brown the meat. Oh, and I'm making a new broccoli casserole."

Leah looked ready to run. "Leah, can you help Grandma get dinner going? I need to check on something." Her eyes told him she knew what he was doing—keeping her there.

"Sure."

He hovered for a second longer than necessary until a smile finally cracked at the edges of her lips. He had every intention of getting the details out of her, but that might prove to be harder than he'd first thought, considering she'd held out this long. And with the way things were going, he'd probably get a SAR callout tonight at the exact wrong time, considering he was on call.

And anyway, why did he think he had a right to her secrets?

With his handgun tucked securely in its holster, he stepped outside and marched around the house to make sure he didn't see any footprints in the melting snow.

When he walked around the front, Terry pulled up the drive in front of the house in his cruiser and climbed out. "I'm off duty now and heading home. See anyone else this week lurking in the shadows?"

"No." Cade glanced back at the house. Somehow he had a feeling that Leah would be very unhappy to see a police officer standing outside. She hadn't gone to the police for a reason. "Just got home myself and was walking the perimeter."

Terry gestured toward the house. "She inside?"

Cade nodded.

"Who is she?" Terry asked.

"I don't know yet."

His eyes narrowed. "You sure know how to pick 'em. You want me to do some checking?"

"No, I think I'm good." Terry was only trying to help. "But maybe drive by once in a while. Maybe seeing the cruiser will keep the lurker away."

Terry agreed and got back in his cruiser to head down the driveway. Cade watched him go, thinking about his offer. He'd rather have Leah tell him, to trust him, than go behind her back that way. The thing was, he wanted to be able to trust her, too, but as much as he was driven to save people who needed saving, to protect Leah, he was hard-pressed to trust her too far. Melissa had forever cured him of trusting easily. But he

didn't have to worry about trusting Leah with
matters of the heart. She had no plans to hang
around that long. Cade didn't want her to go,
but considering how his pulse kicked up a few
notches when he was near her, maybe that was
for the best. But not until he was certain she
was safe.

When Cade went back into the house, the
aroma of Italian cuisine made his mouth water.
Grandma was in the kitchen alone. Cade panicked.

"Where's Leah?"

"She went upstairs to pack, I think."

"What?" Cade grabbed the big pot of pasta
from Grandma and put it on the table.

She pinned him with her gaze. "You were expecting her to stay, dear?"

"Yes," he said. "Yes, I was."

Cade ran up the stairs and knocked on the
door to Leah's room. She opened it and glanced
up at him, her eyes red. He saw the duffel bag
on the bed, but her laptop was open on the desk.
She moved from the door back to her computer.

"Don't go," he said. "I thought we agreed you
would stay and I would help you."

She laughed bitterly. "No, you agreed. I said
nothing."

Leah shut her computer and turned to face
Cade again, pulling back her beautiful hair.

"Look, Cade, I don't want to go, I'll be honest. need a little time to figure things out and…" Sh glanced out the window then back to him. "An then I might survive this. But I won't risk you family. I won't. If you knew what was going on then you wouldn't ask me to stay."

Cade held out his palms. "How can I help i you don't tell me?"

"I don't think you could help even if you knew. Leah sat on the bed, wringing her hands. "I don' even know where to start. It's so complicated."

Cade pulled the chair away from the desk an sat down, holding her gaze. "Start from the be ginning."

"Why did I ever let you talk me into staying? she huffed.

Her turmoil was evident in the twisted fea tures of her face. Cade couldn't stand to see he this way. He wanted to take her in his arms, bu instead took her hand in his. "Leah, it's okay From the sounds of it, you owe it to me to let m in on what's going on."

She nodded. "You're right."

Tears slipped from the corners of her eyes and she wiped at them, sniffling. "I don't usually cry This is embarrassing."

"Nothing wrong with crying. Don't be ashamed."

She gazed up at him, looking unconvinced.

I've seen too much of the world. So many bad things. More than anyone should see."

An ache coursed through him. He didn't know how to help her and that drove him crazy. "Leah…tell me."

"I—"

His pager went off. He grabbed it up and looked, pursing his lips. He'd been afraid this would happen.

Callout SAR for lost snowshoers. Staging point Caryn's Creek. Winter hiking gear needed.

*Unbelievable.* Cade glanced at his watch. It would be dark soon.

"Cade?" Heidi called from the stairs. "Cade?" Her voice drew near as she searched for him.

"In here," he answered.

She paused at Leah's door and looked from Cade to Leah. "You got the callout? I talked to David. They're lost somewhere in the Three Cliffs region."

Heidi waited for Cade to acknowledge that he understood. But he said nothing. He didn't want to desert Leah in the middle of this.

"They're going to need you to assess for this one," Heidi said. "You know that, right? We had all that snow last night." She searched his gaze.

"I'm heading out. You coming?" She didn't wai
for his answer.

Leah squeezed his hand. "Go, you have to go.

He frowned and shook his head. He didn'
want to go this time. He was busy saving some
one else.

"I'll tell you everything when you get back
I...promise." Her eyes confirmed her words.

Could he trust her?

"You never get to eat at normal hours, de
you?" A soft smile played on her lips, breakin;
through her pain.

"Mostly, I do."

He liked her smile, the way her lips hitche
up at the corners in that certain way. It gav
him hope that they were making some headway
And then...then he couldn't help it. He lifted hi
hand and cupped her cheek. Shutting her eyes
Leah leaned into it, close enough for the laven
der scent in her hair to wrap around him, teas
ing him. He could have stayed like that forever
No, he'd much prefer to pull her into his arms
Or maybe even kiss her.

Wait. What was he thinking?

He couldn't do this to her. She was vulner
able and alone. He'd be taking advantage. An
he wouldn't do this to himself. He had to guar
his own heart. If only he didn't feel the nee

o live up to his father's standard of defending
nd protecting.

Swallowing as if he could wash away the knot
n his throat, he let his hand drop. Her startled
yes watched him now. In them, he thought he
ead that she hadn't expected to let her guard
lown, either.

"Listen, I have a friend who's a police officer,"
le said. "He's going to drive by the house once in
. while to show there's a police presence nearby."

Her face visibly paled. "What do you mean?
What did you say to the police?"

"Nothing." Her negative reaction was stronger
han he would have expected and hit him like a
nountain landslide crashing down in his gut. She
vas hiding something from the police.

"Then why?"

He frowned. All things considered, he couldn't
:eep it from her. "There was someone standing
n the woods the first night I brought you here.
Watching."

Her eyes widened, but beyond that she didn't
ippear all that surprised.

"I have to get out of here now. I could have al-
eady been gone if you had told me. Why didn't
/ou tell me? I never should have come here. I
<new that. I've been such an idiot." She started
o head toward her bag, apparently intent on
eturning to packing.

He stood and gripped her shoulders. "Leah wait. Please, I'm begging you, wait until I get back before you do anything rash. You're safe here. Terry's watching the house."

"Me? You're the one who's not safe." Leah tried to break free. "I'm sorry I did this to you."

Cade held tighter. "Promise me that you'll wait until I get back before you leave. Tell me everything, and if I really can't help, then you can go. Besides, Grandma is expecting you for dinner. Please don't disappoint my grandmother."

The hint of a reluctant smile chased away the lines of frustration in her face. Well, most of them anyway.

"I could never disappoint your grandmother. All right. For her sake, and to make sure she is safe, I'll hang around here with her until you get back, but no promises after that."

She stepped closer, acting like she wanted to say more, but was measuring her words first. A battle raged behind her eyes as she hesitated.

Cade waited patiently, though he'd received an urgent callout.

Then finally, she said, "Go. Do what you do best—go save people."

To Cade's surprise, Leah gave him a quick kiss on the lips, then left him standing there and bounded down the stairs.

# TEN

After Cade and Heidi left to find the lost snow-shoers, Katy hovered over her cooking pots and chopped broccoli—the woman seriously enjoyed cooking—and Leah checked the locks on the doors and windows, hoping she'd come across the gun cabinet where Cade kept his weapons.

Discovering a window in Katy's sewing room unlocked, Leah quickly secured it. She peeked through the blinds into the darkness on that side of the house, too far for the security light to do much.

A shudder crawled over her neck and down her back.

Snyder was out there somewhere. She could feel it.

She needed to flip on the outside lights. Was she going crazy to think that he would be bold enough to enter the Warren home? Continuing to check windows, she suddenly realized Katy stood behind her.

"Everything all right, dear?" Katy smiled and adjusted one of her cross-stitched hangings that read "Home is where the heart is."

"Yes, everything's fine." She didn't want to tell Katy about Snyder. Not until she'd told Cade everything. Besides, Katy couldn't do anything but worry, and worry never changed a thing.

"We might as well eat. It could be hours before they return," she said.

Great.

*Please, Cade, hurry back.* Since when had Leah relied on someone besides herself to keep her safe? The answer was simple enough—since the first night she'd stayed in this house.

She followed Katy into the dining room and considered the best way to ask about the location of Cade's weapons. None of this was unfolding the way she'd thought it would.

Cade shouldn't have left, but lives were at stake. Leah should have gone, but she'd had to stay for Katy's sake.

Katy ladled a hefty portion of pasta onto Leah's plate. "I'm so glad you're here to eat with me. The kids are so busy with their own lives— jobs and friends and search and rescue—half the time all my effort to make a nice dinner is wasted."

"Oh, that can't be true," Leah said. "Looks to me like they enjoy all your meals."

They shared small talk as they ate. Leah wondered about Cade's brothers, Adam and David. Maybe they were also involved in the search and rescue tonight. Cade had been called out for avalanche assessment, too, but would help in the search and rescue no doubt. He was so driven when it came to his chosen causes—protecting people from avalanche danger, helping to find and rescue them. She'd never met anyone like him. Some toy maker should create a Cade Warren action figure.

Leah helped Katy clean up their dishes and the kitchen, but kept the pasta and broccoli casserole waiting as the hours seemed to tick slowly by. It had grown dark early, as usual, and was now almost eight-thirty. The SAR team wouldn't stay out there long in the dark, she didn't think, but what did she know about it? With each passing hour, the tension in her shoulders grew. She should never have promised him she would stay, but she couldn't leave his grandmother in the house alone. Not with Snyder out there somewhere. He'd known from the beginning that Leah was staying here, and the thought made her skin crawl. He'd probably wanted to get her alone but she'd never left the house until today.

Leah paced the living room, rubbing her shoulders.

"You worry too much, dear. They'll be all right. You'll see."

She smiled at Katy. The woman had misunderstood Leah's agitation, but Leah had to admit some of her anxiety was for Cade and his siblings. She'd seen firsthand how dangerous their work could be.

"I'm sure you're right." Leah forced a smile. Oh, why had she promised him she'd wait? Promised that she would tell him?

Should she write all the details out and send him an email? Somehow, that didn't feel right. He deserved better.

Standing at the dining-room window at the front of the house, Leah peeked out the mini-blinds. Sure enough, a Mountain Cove PD cruiser crept up the drive and turned around to head back down. If only the sight could make Leah relax rather than remind her of the crazed murderous police detective on her tail. Today she'd intended to purchase some kind of weapon, but that plan had been foiled. Cade had guns in the house somewhere, but she hadn't discovered them yet. Maybe she should find them, and now.

"Would you like some tea, dear?" Katy stood behind her. "On evenings like this, I usually sip my tea and work on my cross-stitch."

"No, thanks. But I think I'll run up to my room

to grab my laptop. I need to do some research. Mind if I join you down here?"

Katy chuckled. "Of course not. I'd enjoy the company."

Leah took one step on the stairs, intending to search for a weapon while she was upstairs. Would Cade keep his guns in his garage apartment? Or in the house somewhere? Leah hated to ask his grandmother, hated to upset her, but safety had to come first. Their lives could be in danger. She should come right out and ask the woman. She sucked in a breath—

The lights went off.

*God, please, no. Not now. Not here.*

"Oh, dear," his grandmother said. "I'm sorry. The power goes off sometimes. We might need to start the generator if it lasts too long. But the glow of the fireplace is light enough for now. Except you can't use the internet. Maybe I should—"

"No," Leah whispered. "Keep quiet."

What if that's all this was? A simple matter of the power going off and not something more. But no, Leah couldn't risk that this was nothing. Where could they hide? How could she protect this woman? In the dim firelight, she spotted the door to the basement. They could hide there and wait it out. Maybe.

"What's wrong?" Katy asked.

Leah rushed to Katy's side and grabbed her hand. She leaned close and whispered into Katy's ear. "Please, listen very carefully. I see you have a basement," she said. "Let's get down there."

"Tell me what's going on." Katy wouldn't move.

"Someone wants to kill me, and I think he might be here." Leah still whispered, but put force behind her words. "Now, let's hide."

"Oh, dear." Katy kept her trembling voice low.

She hurried to the basement door with Leah. Katy jiggled it open, making too much noise. Leah urged the woman through the door and quickly closed it behind them. Right inside the door, Katy grabbed a flashlight hanging on the wall and switched it on. They crept down the steps. At the bottom, Leah glanced up at the door, now in the shadows, wishing it had a lock on it.

Leah turned back to Katy. The woman's face revealed her concern, yet a sense of determination burned there, too.

Katy took the lead and shone the flashlight around. She pointed. "Over there," she whispered. "We can hide behind those plastic storage boxes."

They passed a wall of neatly organized tools and Leah grabbed a wrench. It would have to do.

Leah helped Katy move the storage boxes forward enough for them to crouch behind. Then they waited.

And listened.

Above them, the floor creaked.

Katy flicked the flashlight off. "I can't call the police on my cell. There's no signal down here. I should have—"

"Shh," Leah whispered. She clasped Katy's hand. None of this was the woman's fault. Leah should have been much more prepared. Until this point, this hadn't been Snyder's MO—coming after Leah when she was with someone. Coming into a private home. But his patience had obviously run out.

How far the town hero detective had sunk. Leah squeezed Katy's hand, hoping the woman was praying silently as Leah was.

As soon as this was over, if they lived through it, Leah would leave whether or not Cade had returned. She had to lead Snyder away from Cade's family. Never again would she allow herself to be this vulnerable. The weakness had come when she'd let herself count on someone else. She should have only stayed one night to regroup and get her bearings, plan a new escape, but she'd craved the safety and security, and yes, even the comfort she'd found here. She'd justified her presence here to herself.

Now evil had pursued her, even here, inside what had felt like a fortress. Leah's presence had drawn it inside and put this kind woman at risk.

At the top of the stairs to the basement, the doorknob jiggled. Then the door opened. Pulse soaring, Leah gripped the wrench tighter and held her breath. She suspected Katy held hers, too, instinctively knowing they shouldn't breathe. Shouldn't make even the slightest noise. But Leah thought she could almost hear both their hearts pounding in the silence.

A step groaned above them. He was coming down into the basement. Leah's palms slicked against the wrench. She'd only get one chance at this. She positioned herself for her surprise lunge. She'd have to hit hard.

*God, help me.*

A truck engine rumbled outside and lights flashed through the open door at the top of the stairs, throwing the shadowed silhouette of a man across the opposite wall.

Leah sucked in a breath. Katy grabbed Leah's arm.

Then the shadow froze, turned and ran out.

Katy started to move.

Leah held her back. "Wait."

They couldn't be sure Snyder had left, or even that the person in the truck was someone they could trust. But Leah suspected it was Cade and Heidi returning.

Glass shattered somewhere above them.

*Oh, God, keep Cade and Heidi safe!*

Leah jumped to her feet. If there was any chance that Heidi or Cade was in the vehicle she'd heard approaching, she had to warn them.

Exhaustion overcame Cade as he parked in front of the house.

They'd finally gotten a ping on a cell phone and located the snowshoer who'd gone for help and gotten lost. He helped the rescuers find his buddy who'd fallen and broken his leg. But through all of it, Cade hadn't stopped thinking about Leah. Hadn't stopped thinking about that kiss, though it had been nothing more than quick and innocent. Maybe he'd read more into it, but it had kept him warm the rest of the evening.

Only he wished he'd gotten the information out of her before he'd left, because he'd been distracted during the rescue. Heidi had sensed it, too, and kept grilling him about what was going on, distracting him even more.

She hadn't ridden back with Cade, preferring to hang out with friends. Isaiah had said he'd bring her home. Cade scraped a hand down his scruffy jaw, wondering for not the first time if something was going on between those two.

Something more than the easy friendship they all shared with Isaiah. Cade wasn't sure how he'd feel about that if that were the case. Isaiah was a good man, but Cade suspected he had more than a few secrets.

He turned off the ignition. It suddenly hit him the house was dark, except for the moon peeking through the clouds. Grandma would have started the generator if the power had been out for long.

Cade tensed.

He grabbed his handgun. Quietly, he got out of his truck and approached the house, gun at the ready.

*God, please let this be nothing but a power outage.*

Where was Terry? He thought the guy was supposed to drive by. Probably had other police duties, and driving by Cade's house was unofficial business.

*Lord, please protect my family. Please let them be okay.*

Approaching the door, Cade couldn't decide whether to call out or to keep quiet. The stealth approach won out. He tried the front door.

He unlocked, then slowly opened it. Creeping inside the house, he prayed to God that he didn't fire his weapon at someone he loved. Though his eyes adjusted to the darkness, he could barely see a thing with all the miniblinds closed and curtains drawn. That would be Leah's doing.

What had he been thinking to bring Leah and her troubles back here with him?

When his boots crunched over glass, he heard more than saw someone swinging an object at his head. He ducked and grabbed the wielder in a death grip.

With the whiff of lavender hair, he loosened his grip and turned her around, gripping her arms. "Leah," he whispered.

A curtain whipped open and Cade jumped. Grandma stepped into the light of a moonbeam streaming through the window. "Now we can see. I lost the flashlight down in the basement."

Cade pulled Leah into a hug, relief flooding him. "What happened?"

"Someone was in the house," Grandma answered.

On pure impulse, he'd pulled Leah into his arms and now he wanted to shake her. He released her and stepped away, feeling the absence of her body and warmth to his core, all tangled up with his anger and frustration.

Didn't she have anything to say?

"I'd better check around," he finally said. "Make sure he's gone. I'll get the lights back on."

"He's gone all right. He was almost on us but then you drove up. Leah thought he was still here and that you were him, obviously." Again, Grandma did the talking.

"You didn't call out or say anything, just crept through the door. I'm sorry I tried to take you out," Leah finally spoke up.

"No harm done." What was Cade going to do with this girl?

"I'm calling the police." Grandma sounded shaken.

"No, please, don't," Leah said.

"Give me one good reason why not." Cade had been waiting for hours to hear what Leah would tell him. He was done waiting.

"I don't trust them, that's why."

"I've known Terry since I was in grade school."

"You trust him more than you trust me. I get that. Call him. But leave me out of it."

*Oh, she was part of it, all right.*

Cade called 9-1-1 and relayed to dispatch they'd had an intruder. He eyed Leah, who stared at him with her arms crossed. She rubbed them. Nervous or cold, he wasn't sure. If only he could have stayed to hear her story, these two women he cared so much about might not have been in danger. It didn't escape his notice that he'd lumped Leah in with Grandma as someone he cared about.

He couldn't deny that he'd grown attached to

...er in a short time. But he might have to claim insanity on that one.

Cade finished checking the house and restored the power. A simple matter of flipping the main breaker. It might be a bit before a police cruiser showed up. There could be another emergency tonight, and the Warren household was out of danger at the moment.

While Grandma warmed up the spaghetti dinner he'd missed, he grabbed Leah's arm and dragged her out of earshot so they could speak in private. Grandma had given him the eye, meaning she expected him to find out what was going on. Not because she was angry with Leah. No, his grandmother didn't have an angry bone in her body. Grandma would want Cade to do a better job of protecting the girl his grandmother thought was "a dear."

But Cade was angry at himself. He'd known there'd been someone watching the house that first night and still he'd insisted she stay. He was angry at Leah for putting them all in danger. He shoved away his frustrations. No time for that. He needed details. Staying calm, being patient, would get him more answers. Maybe if he could disconnect his emotions from her somehow, he could think through this whole thing with clarity.

Looking at her now, he thought of her quick

kiss again. And all his anger melted away. No good. He was entirely too vulnerable.

"Tell me," he said.

Tears streamed from her eyes. In the short time he'd known her, he'd seen nothing but how strong she was—until today. He thought her knees might buckle, but then she bent over, and Cade tucked her in his arms, bearing her up. He brushed his hand down the back of her soft mane of blond hair.

When he sensed she had regained her composure, he urged her into a chair in the corner of the room.

"Tell me." He pinned her with his gaze. "I won't let him hurt you."

Men who abused women were the lowest creatures on earth, but to break into his house and send his grandmother into hiding in the basement along with Leah, the man had found a new enemy.

Leah wiped at her nose. He grabbed a tissue and handed it to her. "I'm sorry if I sounded angry, but I need to know what this is all about."

She hung her head. "You have every right to be angry with me. I'm such an idiot for staying here for even one minute. I thought…I needed a safe place to hide while I figured things out."

Cade couldn't stand it anymore. He crouched down to look up into her face. "If you need a safe place to stay, then you've found it. You can stay as long as you like, but I need to know what I'm dealing with here."

She nodded. "I'm sorry I didn't tell you before. I thought that I was protecting you because if you know what I know, then you could be in danger."

He grabbed her wrists, making her look at him. "You see we're already in danger."

She took in a shuddering breath. "I witnessed murder."

*Whoosh.*

Her words were a punch in the gut. He hadn't expected that, but he remained where he was. Let her know he was there for her. He'd expected to hear she had an abusive ex tracking her down. But…a murderer? This was out of his league.

No matter. Cade would do the right thing. He'd do whatever was within his power to help her.

"Then why would you run? Why didn't you tell the police?"

"This is where it gets complicated. The guy who murdered my boss is a decorated town hero. A detective in the police department. Now do you see?"

Cade blew out a breath. "You didn't think anyone would believe you?"

She shook her head, shoved from the chair and paced. "Of course not. I didn't think I would survive long enough to tell anyone. I think that's what happened to Tim—my boss, the man who was killed. He found something on Snyder. That's why he'd insisted I leave for a vacation. Only he didn't tell me any of this. But when I saw Snyder kill him, I got out of town as fast as I could. Kept my travel low key. But he found me anyway. How, I have no idea."

"Okay. So you saw this guy kill your boss. Then you disappeared. Didn't you think the authorities would immediately suspect you killed him? Oh, wait. Is that why you avoided the hospital? You didn't want your name in their system in case the cops decided to look for you?"

"Obviously, I've been found out by the cop I'm trying to avoid, so it's too late for that. Snyder is overseeing this murder case from his end. Don't you see? He doesn't want anyone else to question me."

"How do you know he's on the case?" he asked.

Leah frowned. "He's a hero in Kincaid. If he wants a case, he gets it. I knew he'd want this one. Besides, I read his comments about the case online. He's the detective in charge." She managed a laugh. "He even commented about me stating I wasn't currently a person of interest because I was on a cruise in the Caribbean."

"A cruise?"

"Yeah." Leah shuddered. "I was heading ou

f town for the cruise when I went in late to grab omething. I saw it all in the parking garage."

"This is bad." Cade shook his head. "Very ad."

"But I didn't go on that cruise. I changed my lans to mix things up. Came to the only place could think of where he couldn't find me. Tim nherited the cabin recently so I knew all about . I took the ferry. Sure, the detective could pin ne with the murder, but first he wants what he ninks I have. Then he'll dispose of me. It's eas- er for him if I simply disappear. He thinks if e threatens me, I'll give it up. That I'll believe e'll let me live."

Cade stood, too. She stared out the window ow. He wanted to pull her into his arms again. Does this have anything to do with the witness t the avalanche?"

"Yes. That was him. He was on the mountain. 'hreatened me with a knife. Wanted what I sup- osedly have. I was running from him when the valanche hit. He was dressed as you described ne witness. I can't know if he had someone with im or not. There may still be a victim under the now, but I doubt it."

"What do you have that he wants, Leah?"

"I don't know. Maybe he thinks I ended up vith the evidence against him that Tim had." She urned to him then, red and blue lights flashing

across her face in the window. "Please, Cade
Don't tell the police any of this. I don't know
who I can trust with this information. Do you
understand?"

"How can I help you? What do you need to
solve this?"

"I need to go back to Washington, to Kincaid.
Dread flickered in her gaze. "I need to go back
to Tim's office."

# ELEVEN

Leah stared out the window of the floatplane Cade had secured through a bush pilot friend— guy named Billy—to transport them. It had been two days since Snyder had broken into the house, but it had taken them that long to arrange everything. Leah was all too aware that she was running out of time.

Cade knew the people and had connections that Leah didn't. He'd become an asset she hadn't known she would need.

When Snyder had found her, she thought she'd made a big mistake in going to the cabin. But meeting Cade had changed her mind. Now she believed God had led her here, after all. With Cade's hand gripping the armrest, she wanted to reach out and lay her hand over his. Let him know how grateful she was that God had sent him.

The small plane flew over a ferry like the one Leah had taken to get here. She wished she could

have taken that amazing trip without the burde
of the murder she'd witnessed. Without the fea
of being tracked. As she watched the snowcappe
mountains, rainforest islands and waters of th
Inside Passage beneath them through the wir
dow, she wondered how she'd let Cade talk he
into letting him come along. It was one thing
stay at his house a few days, but another for hir
to get involved in her search for answers.

For all practical purposes, she was a fugitiv

The night Snyder had broken into the hous
she'd overheard Cade's conversation with h
grandmother and sister when he'd told them he
be going with her to Washington. They hadr
understood why he'd go this far to help Leah,
woman none of them knew well enough to trus
Leah wasn't sure why he was doing so much, e
ther. At least Cade had insisted the two wome
stay with his aunt and uncle—his father's si
ter—for a few days. They'd left earlier, takir
the three-day ferry to Seattle, which should p
plenty of time and space between them and Sn
der.

Isaiah and Adam, and even David if necessar
could handle the Mountain Cove Avalanche Ce
ter until Cade and Heidi were back.

Leah had no idea if Snyder knew they had lef
or if he would guess where they were headed. I
had a job to do, too, and couldn't afford to tal

o much time off to harass Leah. He couldn't
ford to raise more suspicions. Maybe he would
aim he was investigating Tim's murder. Of
ourse, his methods were not sanctioned by any
w-enforcement entity.

Regardless, there was a piece missing in the
ay Snyder was handling things. Why was he
king so long to make any real move against
er? Why was he playing games?

In leaving Mountain Cove, she and Cade had
ade sure they hadn't been followed. Bottom
ne, she'd never be free of Snyder, nor would
e survive, if she didn't find out what was going
n. She'd made a few discoveries that left her
ith theories, but she needed hard-copy files
om Tim's office to go through his client list for
e past several years. See if any others besides
e three had died. She had no idea if she was
n the wrong track, but it was a start.

Shutting her eyes, she pinched the bridge of
er nose. *Oh, Tim, why didn't you leave me a
'ue?* He'd thought he'd been protecting her by
nding her away—she got that now—but in the
d, by keeping her in the dark, his nightmare
ad become hers.

A hand brushed hers then grabbed two of her
ngers. Leah turned to look into Cade's eyes. It
minded her of that day on the medevac helicop-
r when he'd ridden next to her. He smiled. She'd

liked his smile the first time she'd seen it. He
been looking down at her when he'd uncovere
the snow from her face where she'd been burie
in the avalanche. His smile had been meant
reassure, yet he'd done so much more. He wa
beginning to mean so much to her, and that te
rified her.

"Are you okay?" he asked.

She blinked. Where did she start? She didn
want him to be involved. Hated that she'd pr
him and his family in danger. And yet, wher
would she be right now without him? "Sure.
guess I'm wondering why you would do this fr
me."

A frown crept into his smile. "Did you expe
me to just let you go? To stand by and do notl
ing while you were in danger? You didn't as
for this to happen. And neither did I, but we'
both in it now."

Leah nodded. She understood him better tha
he knew. "I know you're trying to be the her
again, but you can't control everything in lif
Sometimes, you can't save people. Sometime
all you can do is surrender."

Hurt flickered across his mountain-green ey
and Leah instantly regretted her words.

"You mean give up. I'm not willing to do that
Even his attempt at a smile couldn't hide his di
appointment at her words. "It can't hurt to d

me digging. And this way, I know you're safe.
don't have to worry that something happened
o you."

That he'd worry about her that way—the idea
made heat shoot through that cold, hard place in
er heart. She had no idea how to respond. Be-
ides her mother, no one had cared about her like
his. No one had risked so much for her.

"Thank you," Leah whispered. Tears welling,
he turned to look out the window so he couldn't
ee her cry.

Once they arrived in Juneau they took an
Alaska Airlines flight to SeaTac, landing at the
eattle-Tacoma International Airport.

The next few hours would be tricky, if not
arrowing, but the intense pressure of a tick-
ng clock weighed on her. At some point Sny-
er would give up on getting what he wanted
rom her, and he'd pin Tim's murder on her and
et a warrant for her arrest. Deal with her that
vay. And once he figured out that she didn't
ven have whatever it was he wanted, she was
s good as dead.

As they disembarked from the jet, the truth
inally hit her, stealing her breath. If it was evi-
ence that Snyder wanted, then he had to know
he didn't have it, or she would have already
urned Snyder in.

Snyder wanted *her* to find it for *him*. How could she have been so stupid?

As they headed along the Jetway to the terminal, Leah slowed. Cade glanced back, worry lining his face. He reached for her, tugging her behind him as he moved with the flow of bodies.

Every airport security guard she and Cade passed sent icy fear through her veins. They followed the signs to baggage claim. In the distance a man stood at a newsstand.

Snyder!

Leah grabbed Cade's hand and ducked into a nook. Heart in her throat, she struggled to breathe.

"What is it?" he asked.

"Snyder. He's here." Leah covered her mouth, holding back the panic.

"Where?"

"He was buying something at a newsstand."

"Leah." Cade tipped her chin up, his eyes locking with hers. "We have to act normally. Not draw attention. If he was waiting or watching for us, he would have been standing there when we walked out. My guess is he's getting ready to board the plane we exited and head back."

Cade leaned against the wall next to Leah and blew out a breath. "Let's head into the store at the corner of this alcove. I'm going to buy a base ball cap, at least. You need something over your head, too."

"There," Leah whispered. "He's…over there."

Cade turned sideways, his back to Snyder, to shield Leah with his body and hide her. "We need to act like a couple until we get out of here."

When his gaze flicked to her lips, something warm surged inside. Leah remembered that moment she'd given him a quick kiss. She wasn't sure what had come over her, but she'd been overcome with emotion for this man. She still was, no matter how hard she tried to hold it back.

Cade ran his thumb down her cheek. He was only acting the part, she reminded herself, but when his gaze roamed back up and focused on her eyes, she knew she saw something more behind them. And that current had been there all along between them, but Leah had ignored it because she couldn't afford to fall for someone. She stepped away from him, disconnecting whatever flowed between them.

When they caught sight of Snyder walking away from the area, they entered the store to make their purchases and then headed to the terminal exit. Cade held her close, as though they were a couple. Other than dressing grunge, as if they were much younger, that was their only disguise. The funny thing was, she fit perfectly against him, his arm wrapped around her.

Her chest tightened. She couldn't let herself fall for him. She'd never met a man she could trust, and here she was trusting this man with everything. They walked right by baggage claim and strolled to the vehicle rental booths. Leah pulled away, wanting some distance. This was for show, she reminded herself, but her heart wasn't buying it. And she had to protect her heart at all costs.

Cade rented a vehicle for them. They decided she should leave her car where it was parked at the airport. Keep up whatever ruse was left.

"Which way?" he asked, the Seahawks baseball cap he'd purchased in the airport tugged low.

"For starters, I know an out-of-the-way hole-in-the-wall that makes great chili." She hunkered low in the seat. "We need to wait to go to the office until it's dark and quiet and nobody's around. As it was when Tim was murdered."

Cade didn't like it.

He didn't like it at all. They'd killed a few hours in Seattle. Eaten the chili. But now they were heading to the outskirts, into Kincaid where they would get down to the dirty business of slinking into a murdered man's office.

He glanced at Leah, then turned his focus back to steering the vehicle as it crept along the lonely streets.

The conversation he'd had with Heidi and Grandma drifted back to him. He couldn't argue that he was out of his element with this sort of task, but he also couldn't leave Leah to do this on her own. He understood her reasoning—she had to find out what this guy was after other than her life. It was the only way.

Her only path to freedom.

"Ready?" she asked.

*Nope.* He nodded.

"We'll eat at the diner across from the office, wait and watch. Make sure Snyder doesn't have a flunky monitoring the building."

"Chances are he'll figure out we're not in Mountain Cove soon, if he hasn't already." Cade edged into a parking space and turned off the ignition. Shifted to look at Leah.

"Yeah, but will he think we came back here?" she asked.

"That's the billion-dollar question." Cade climbed out.

He ushered Leah into the diner, both pretending they were relaxed. Both likely failing. Ultra aware of his surroundings, Cade looked over the other customers. He hadn't ever hung out in a diner at two in the morning, but apparently it was the hopping place for night owls.

They chose a corner booth that afforded a good view of the street. Each ordered coffee and a short stack, but Cade wasn't hungry. He doubted Leah was, either. They tried to act normal.

Leah hadn't disclosed much more with Cade than that she'd witnessed her boss's murder and she was searching for answers. They'd had plenty of travel time to talk about things, but she hadn't offered any additional info and he hadn't pushed.

Now that he was here, sharing in this with her, he was almost beginning to second-guess the decision to come. He'd never in his life done anything so clandestine. But then he'd never met anyone in Leah's situation. He understood why she needed to get into her old office, Tim's office, during the middle of the night so no one would see her.

But Cade recognized that he needed to know more—such as details and a plan. His gaze darted around, making sure no one would hear their conversation. The diner was noisy and there wasn't anyone sitting near.

He leaned in. "What are we looking for, Leah?"

"He could have killed me already," she whispered.

That wasn't an answer to his question, but at least she was talking. "So what are you saying? That he doesn't want to?"

The waitress brought their breakfast, balancing the dishes like a plate spinner in a circus act.

When she left, Leah continued. "Oh, he wants to. But so far he can't afford to kill me until he gets whatever he's looking for. Then all bets are off."

"Right. You'd be the only loose end he has left." These were things Cade already knew.

Leah didn't act as though she'd heard him. Over the brim of her coffee mug, she was watching something through the window.

Cade followed her gaze. Someone in a dark overcoat jaywalked, crossing over to the old bank building that Cade and Leah would soon enter. He held his breath as the person walked by the parking garage and then the entrance and kept walking another block. Ignoring the flashing Don't Walk signal, he crossed without looking both ways. Cade took a sip of his black coffee. He was going to need it.

"You're a legal investigator. What's your take on all this? You must have some idea of what he wants from you."

She dragged in a breath. "I worked for Tim for two years. It was my two-year anniversary in fact. He was keeping something from me, and I suspected he was sending me away for a three-week vacation to keep me out of it."

"To protect you?"

"Cade, you should know something about me. I don't...trust people."

No surprise there. Cade kept his thoughts to himself on that one.

"Life hasn't given me a reason to trust anyone except God."

Funny, she trusted God but not people. He had more struggles with God. Why He chose to save some people and let others die. Like his father.

"I was set to leave that night," she said. "I was going to Florida to visit my aunt, and then I planned to take a Caribbean cruise. I'd gotten a late start and stopped by the office on the way out. Tim had given me a necklace—sort of two year anniversary, hooray-for-me gift—and I left it. Forgot it. I felt bad later when I realized I'd left it behind and thought I'd grab it so I wouldn't hurt his feelings. But the truth is, I also wanted to catch him in… I don't know, whatever he was hiding from me. I wanted to look around the office, to see if I could find something. I figured that if he thought I was gone maybe he'd relax and leave something on his desk."

Cade downed his coffee. "And you saw the murder instead."

Leah played with her fork. "Yeah, that. I have a theory about why he killed Tim, but maybe I'm wrong. Maybe Tim was involved with Snyder and double-crossed him."

"Is it impossible to think that your boss found

something out about Snyder? Maybe he planned to expose him and didn't want you in the cross-fire. Oh, wait. That's your theory, isn't it?"

"Yes. It's the obvious first choice of theories, if you want to take the high road." Her blue-green eyes studied him. "Do you always look for the good in people?"

"Why shouldn't I?"

"I don't have an answer for that," she said. "I'm with you, by the way. I think Tim had planned to expose him, and wanted to keep me out of it. Obviously that plan backfired. But to answer your question, I'm looking for anything I can find. Maybe I'll know it when I see it. More specifically, I need to look at files on all of Tim's clients. The ones who Tim got off, the ones who didn't go to prison."

A police cruiser crept down the street. Leah ducked her head and focused on her cold pancakes.

Cade tugged his cap lower and leaned back into the corner of the booth against the window. "This feels wrong."

"You can get out any time you want."

"No, I mean that we have to act like this. To hide from the police like they're the bad guys. But until we know more, unfortunately they are—at least in Kincaid."

She nodded. "Could be someone working with Snyder, watching the building on his orders."

"Then when he's out of sight we need to get inside."

"The good news is that Snyder is likely in Mountain Cove while we're here." She smiled this time.

One of these days, when this was over, he hoped to see her smile all the time. She was the strongest woman he'd ever met, and she deserved a few reasons to smile. Why was he thinking long-term? Maybe because part of him wanted something long-term with this woman. The other part remembered what Melissa had done to him.

The cruiser parked and the police officer strolled into the diner. He scanned the room then sat in a corner that gave him a clear view of the street.

Great. How were they going to get inside the building without him noticing?

"We should go," Leah said.

"No. Wait." Cade ordered more coffee. "We leave when we've finished with our breakfast. Act normal. You need to relax. Leaving now would look suspicious." Maybe. He didn't know. He hadn't done this before.

"What if he recognizes me?"

"Is there a warrant out for your arrest? Or is your picture circulating as a person of interest?"

The waitress poured them more coffee then took care of her other patrons. Cade leaned forward. "A better question is, do you recognize him?"

She shook her head. Cade had two more cups of coffee. He needed to be more alert than he'd ever been tonight. He already felt naked without a weapon, especially in this situation.

He glanced at the bill the waitress had left. "It's time."

Leah's look asked him what he was doing calling the shots. He shrugged.

She slid from the booth. Cade stood and dropped enough money to cover their breakfast and a few extra dollars for a tip. They continued with a fake conversation, blending in with the diner crowd that had unfortunately thinned.

Cade wished they had parked in a dark alley so they could walk away into the night. Instead the officer could look up the license plate of Cade's rental if he wanted to. Find something out. How had Cade so quickly fallen into this pattern of thinking?

But this was life and death. How he wished he could have told Terry. See what he knew— if anything—about this Snyder character. Cade shifted into Reverse and backed from the parking spot. With Snyder making frequent trips to

Mountain Cove, someone had to have seen him. Struck up a conversation.

"Now where? If we park in the shadows, that officer is going to recognize this vehicle when he makes his rounds." Cade steered slowly down the street.

"Then we need to be quick about it," she said.

"What are you saying?" He seemed to be asking that question a lot, though oddly enough, he understood her all too well most of the time. Maybe if he hadn't connected with her so instantly, he wouldn't have sensed something was wrong. He wouldn't have offered her refuge, and he wouldn't even be here with her now.

"We need to get in and out before he's back to making his rounds," she said.

Whipping off his cap, he ran one hand through his hair while he managed the wheel with the other. If this ended badly, he would definitely never live up to his father's reputation. But somehow Cade doubted that his father would have let Leah down, either. And that thought brought a measure of relief.

Leah directed him to park a few blocks over. They headed back on foot, walking past dark nooks and corners. They crossed the street from the other side of the building, more difficult to see from the diner. Cade caught a glimpse of the parking lot, though.

"The cruiser is gone," he said.

"This way." She hurried into the parking garage. "Careful of the security cameras. They're at each corner."

"Why didn't the cameras catch the murder, Leah?"

"Why do you think? They can't cover the whole garage. It must have been a blind spot."

"But the police would have seen you there that night. The cameras would have caught you watching—very clearly not holding a gun or standing over the body, right?"

Her gaze speared him. "The police? You mean Snyder? He's the detective on the case, remember? He made sure of it so he could stay on top of the cameras and other details."

Her patience with him was wearing thin, but she'd had more time to think this through than he had.

Leah used a key card to enter the building and they got on an elevator. She pulled latex gloves from her pocket and slid them on. Looking at Cade, she shrugged. "They'll know I was here by the key-card log if they decide to dig that deep. My fingerprints are probably on everything, but they won't be on anything new, or anything Snyder might have planted to use against me as a murder weapon if I were to accidentally touch it." She handed a pair over to Cade. "Here."

Wow. She'd thought things through to the nth degree. He frowned, hating every minute of this. What other surprises could he expect? She touched the fourth-floor button.

When the elevator beeped and the door whooshed open, Cade's palms grew moist inside the gloves.

Leah grabbed his hand and tugged him out. "Relax, you're not doing anything illegal. This is my office. I work here, remember?"

Yeah, in the middle of the night wearing latex gloves. "At least, until your boss was murdered."

Cade wished he'd kept that thought to himself. He followed Leah down the hallway. He didn't see any security cameras. *What have you gotten yourself into?* The second elevator on the floor dinged. Someone had followed them up.

# TWELVE

The office of Tim Levins, attorney-at-law, was only five steps away.

Pulse pounding in her ears, Leah focused on the doorknob. The keyhole. With the gloves, she fumbled with the key. What was wrong with her?

She could do this. Had to do this.

*Come on, come on, come on.*

Who would be here at this hour? The officer from the diner come to arrest them? Security checking each floor? She didn't recall someone doing that in the past, but that was before there'd been a murder in the parking garage.

Panic lodged in her throat.

Leah thrust the key in.

At the same time she opened the door, the elevator door opened, resounding into the silent hallway.

*God, please make us invisible.*

Cade rushed inside behind her.

He gently urged the door shut, managing to

avoid the expected latching noise made when the tongue hit the strike plate. The door was mahogany but the wall on either side was glass. Cade and Leah flattened themselves against the door. hiding. Waiting for whoever was on the floor to leave. They saw a flashlight beam through the window on one side of the door and flashed around. Cade tugged Leah over and out of the way. Then the light shone through on the other side.

Had to be security checking the floors, especially after the murder.

Leah held her breath until the guard moved on.

"I thought you said we weren't doing anything illegal," Cade whispered in her ear, his warm breath cascading down her neck.

"We're not." She kept her voice equally low.

Was he messing with her? He knew exactly why she didn't want to be seen by the wrong party coming in or out of this office. Coming in or out of this city.

Finally the security guard made his way down the hall. They waited, listening until they heard the elevator once again. Cade stood close to her. Much too close. She looked up, his strong jaw mere inches from her face. His broad shoulders and muscular biceps were right there.

In her face.

Next to her.

Then she gazed up and caught him watching her with his mountain-green eyes. The man made her heart tumble over itself. When this was over...

When this was over—*what*? She and Cade could be together? Explore a relationship? What would it be like to be loved by a man like Cade? But Leah could never, *ever*, let herself do that. It was too hard to trust after everything she'd witnessed and been through. Too hard to take Cade at face value. She hadn't even known men like Cade existed.

She slipped around him to escape.

"I need to search Tim's office," she said. "But no lights. Those can be seen from the street. And we don't want that in case anyone is watching. I'll use the flashlight." She grabbed one from inside the receptionist's desk and held it up. "Sheila has a drawer full of everything."

"What do you want me to do?" Cade asked.

"Stand guard."

Cade frowned. "I could help you look. Get us out of here faster."

"No. You wouldn't know what to look for. Please, just stand guard for us. Snyder has probably cleaned everything important out of here already—that is, what he could clean up without raising suspicion."

*That's one reason why he wants me search-*

*ing for the evidence Tim found.* But she wouldn'
share that with Cade. He was already freaked
out as it was.

"Then why are we here, risking so much?"

"In case he missed something or left what I
need to figure this out." Leah left Cade in the
reception area to watch the hallway.

He didn't look happy, but she couldn't help
it. She slipped into Tim's office and flicked the
blinds closed before turning on the flashlight.
Tim had a set protocol for documentation and client files, both hard and digital copy. Inactive or
active, copies had been made of all files so they
could be quickly turned over to clients if needed

First she scanned the room. Nothing looked
out of place, but no doubt *Detective* Snyder had
already been over it with a high-powered micro-
scope. If she didn't find anything that jumped ou
at her in here, she'd move to the closed case files
kept in the extra office, and she needed Tim's attorney notes. Tim had been in the process of se-
curing a storage service company to inventory
the files in case he needed the paperwork down
the road, but it was currently all still in the office

Leah sagged under the weight of it all. She
didn't have the time she needed to figure this out

"Come on, Tim, why did he kill you? Wha
does Snyder want from me?" She'd wanted to
think the best of Tim, but maybe it wasn't like

that at all. Maybe Tim was involved in something illicit and that's why he'd wanted her gone—so she wouldn't catch on.

Leah strolled around the office, looking. Tim's laptop was gone, but the desktops remained. Snyder would have had his computer geek comb through the computers, but obviously, he hadn't found what he needed.

*God, please help me to find out what is going on here.*

She tugged file cabinets open and flipped through the files. She didn't have time to write all the names down. She rummaged through his desk. Even broke into two drawers that were locked. No doubt they'd already been sifted through. Frustration was getting the best of her.

On the top of one of the filing cabinets was the box filled with old letters, bills and scraps of papers Tim had brought from the cabin. She sifted through. Nothing important, except…wait. She skimmed a couple of the old letters. Arguments. Apologies. There might be something in here to help Cade with his search for answers about his father. She'd take this with her.

Setting the box on the desk, she flopped back in Tim's chair. She'd read through this first, so Cade wouldn't unnecessarily get his hopes up.

Cade stuck his head around the door. "Find anything?"

Shaking her head, she stood and walked by Cade, heading to her own office.

"Then we need to leave before we get caught even though we're not doing anything…illegal."

Leah ignored him and pushed the door to her office open. Cade followed her inside. Backing onto the conference room that spanned the outside walls, her office had no windows. She flipped on the desk lamp.

"Maybe we should talk about it," he said. "If you tell me what happened, maybe you'll think of something. Tell me about the cabin. Why did you choose the cabin to hide? First you told me a friend was letting you stay there. Then you told me Tim sent you to investigate, but neither of those statements is true. I'm not calling you a liar, don't worry, I understand you didn't know who you could trust."

Leah sank into her chair. Cade found the one in the corner next to her fake tree. "Tim inherited the place months ago. He wanted me to go check it out, and I was scheduled to do that, but he changed his mind and went to see it himself.

"When I saw him killed, I panicked. Didn't know where to go. I remembered the cabin. There was no paper trail to tie it to me, so it seemed like the perfect place to hide. I went to the airport and parked my car in long-term parking as though I still planned to go to Florida. I took a cab to the ferry and then I took the ferry to Alaska instead where I bought a clunker SUV to get around. Paid cash for it all. I wanted to disappear."

She sank lower in the seat. She would never escape this. Never.

"Then what happened?"

"Snyder found me there and chased me up the mountain. There was an avalanche. You know the rest."

"No, I mean after Tim came back from the cabin. Did anything strange happen?"

Leah was an experienced investigator. She shouldn't need Cade's prodding, but then, her mind was messed up at the moment.

"He'd been acting strange all along, as though he was hiding something. It's my job to read people. To know when they're being evasive or deceptive. That's when he sent me packing for a three-week vacation." She opened the drawer and pulled out the necklace, holding it up. "Gave me this memento from his trip to Alaska. I got a bonus, too."

Tears crept from the corners of her eyes as she looked at the pendant of quartz etched in gold hanging from the silver chain. Leah wiped them away. She tried to put on the necklace, but her hands shook too much.

"Here, let me."

Leah stood so Cade could put it on her. She wasn't sure why she wanted to wear it now. It was a little late for that. But she hadn't appreciated it the way she should have, her suspicious mind running away with her, wondering why Tim wanted her out of his way.

"There." Cade had fastened the necklace.

"You shouldn't be here. You shouldn't have come with me." Unshed tears in her voice gave her away. "I'm sorry I involved you."

He turned her to face him and tipped her chin up. "I thought we'd been over that already." He cupped her cheeks.

Leah could swear he was going to kiss her.

How could she want him to kiss her so much? What was wrong with her? They were in the middle of finding the cure to a malignancy that was eating her alive and she wanted this man to kiss her?

"We're in this together and I'm not going to leave your side."

Stupid tears again.

She wiped them away and stared at this man who said he wouldn't leave her. And if she was as good at reading people as she thought, he wasn't lying. Oh, how she wanted to believe him. She'd never wanted anything more in her life, and yet, she had never trusted another soul with so much.

Her existence. Her life. Her heart… No, not that. Never that.

Cade inched forward and joined his lips with ers. Soft. Reassuring. Not taking. Only giving. He was a rock. A pillar she could lean on. And eah took in all the strength she could. That a iss could make so much difference astounded er. He'd known exactly what she needed.

How?

This was so much more than simple attrac-on. What, she wasn't really sure. Her need to nd out battled with internal warnings of im-ninent danger.

Leah could never risk so much.

Beautiful Leah had somehow enchanted him. rawn him into her cloak-and-dagger world. He ulled away, just a little. Her pliant body snapped attention, her partially lidded gaze growing ide.

Cade sucked in a breath, expecting the worst. If she slapped him, he would deserve it.

But he wouldn't lie to himself. He'd thought bout kissing her from the moment he'd pulled er from the snow.

And here he was, kissing a girl in the middle f the best part of the espionage thriller their ves had become, turning things all sappy. But ne'd needed reassurance, and for the first time

in his life, Cade had no idea how to deal with i
How to give what was needed. Instead he'd ju
done what had felt right.

He took a step back and removed his ca
shoving a hand through his hair. He wouldn
apologize. Saying he was sorry would be a li
too. If anything, he needed to get the kiss out o
the way. He'd confirmed that she'd felt the con
nection between them, too.

In some perverse way, it satisfied his need t
know that he was doing the right thing, eve
though he was getting in deep with a woman h
barely knew.

"Okay." She cleared her throat. "I need to g
the box I left in Tim's office and we need to g
out of town."

Her sagging demeanor told him she was mo
than disappointed that she hadn't found what sh
was looking for, and he didn't know what else h
could do. Wait— Yes. Yes, he did. It was tin
to pull his friend Terry into this. Terry woul
listen and know what to do. Leah wouldn't lik
the suggestion, so Cade would keep it to hin
self until he figured out how to present his cas
Surely she knew she was running out of option

Whatever happened, Cade knew he had t
stand between her and Snyder. She leaned ove
to turn off the desk lamp. The necklace hun
forward, catching the light.

Something strangely familiar drifted in and out of Cade's awareness.

The light off, Leah moved past him, bearing her flashlight.

"Wait," he said, catching her wrist.

"I don't have time for—"

"The necklace. Let me see it again." Cade turned the light back on. He examined the gold-etched quartz.

Standing far too close to Leah made it hard for him to focus on the necklace, considering the kiss they'd shared moments ago.

"What's the matter?" she asked.

"Let me get a closer look in good lighting. Take it off." Cade slipped behind her to unclasp it and thrust it beneath the light. "I see this every day. I know exactly what this is."

Her gaze rose up to meet his. "You see gold quartz every day? Where?"

"Not the quartz. I see maps every day. It's a topographical map. The contour lines, marking the elevations, is why I recognized that it was a map."

Leah gasped, covering her mouth with both hands, her eyes squinting to see the small markings.

Cade grinned. "I think we got what we came for."

She met his gaze. "If you hadn't come with

me, I wouldn't have seen this. I wouldn't hav
realized what it really is."

"We can celebrate later. Let's get out of here.

"Wait. I thought of something." She stroke
her forehead. "I can't believe I didn't think c
this before. It could be something, but mayb
it's nothing. And maybe Tim would have hid
den this from me."

"Well, what is it?" Cade felt an urgent need t
get out of this place. They'd found something
Now they had to go.

She weaved her hair back from her face. "W
have a file check-out system we use so we knov
who has which file. Tim and I have handled ev
erything while Sheila is out on maternity leave
She's due back to work next week. I'm so gla
she was at home during all of this. Maybe all
need is to see what client files Tim has checke
out over the past few weeks. Then I can cross-re1
erence them with Detective Snyder, to see whic
cases he handled. See how it is all related."

"Sounds like a plan. Now let's get out of here.

They exited Leah's office and she grabbed th
box from Tim's desk. "The check-out list is a
Sheila's desk."

Cade grabbed Leah's hand, weaving his fir
gers with hers, and headed down the hallwa
into the reception area. Cade suddenly realize

he had neglected to stand guard. They'd both gotten caught up in the search.

They stepped into the reception area.

A man pointed a gun at Leah's head.

# THIRTEEN

"Don't move." The man flashed a badge. "Kin caid Police."

A silencer was attached to the gun barrel.

Leah didn't have time to think, to react, be fore Cade shoved her into the hallway. An in stant later a bullet hit the wall somewhere behind them. Then another.

The muted gunfire still sounded like a weapon had been fired off, but at least it wasn't as deaf ening as it would have without the sound sup pressor. And likely no one else in the building or on the street had heard the gunshots.

But a policeman shooting a gun with a si lencer? *I don't think so.*

An officer shooting at them? *Nope.*

If they ran, he'd give chase, but he wouldn' shoot. They weren't even armed.

Cade practically carried her into Tim's office He slammed the door, locked it and shoved the desk in front of it, before the guy slammed into the door from the other side.

"What are you doing?" she hissed.

"Get down." He pushed her behind the filing cabinets. "Stay there."

"Where would I go? We're trapped in here, thanks to you."

Pressed against the wall, he scanned the room. "I need a weapon. Don't happen to have one hidden away in here, do you?"

"No, I lost my only gun on the mountain."

He frowned, looking nothing like a man in control.

The threat on the other side of the door fired off several rounds, shredding the door.

"The fire escape," Leah whispered. Good thing they were in Tim's office and not hers.

"Make it happen," Cade said. "I'll take care of him."

Predictably the man thrust his fist through the door where he'd concentrated his bullets, creating a hole. He shoved at the desk then aimed his weapon at Leah. How many more rounds did he have? She ducked, Cade grabbed the man's arm and slammed it across the desk at an angle. The cracking sound and resulting wail sent a pang through her.

The gun slid across the desk.

She opened the window and peeked out.

Where were the real police when you needed them? She glanced back at Cade who nodded for her to go ahead, and caught a glimpse of the man on the other side of the big gash in door. Not much of a look, but she could search the police department pictures. See if he was an officer working with Snyder.

Cade moved the desk, which brought Leah back through the window. "What are you doing?"

"Go!"

Leah slipped out the window again and onto the fire escape, for the first time grateful Tim's office was in an older building. A cold gust whipped around her body and she tugged the hood back over her head. She hoped Cade would hurry, because this was freaking her out.

She made it down the first flight of stairs and was halfway on the second. *Oh, God, please, let Cade be right behind me. Help us.*

Then she saw him, taking the wrought-iron fire escape steps much faster than Leah had and catching up with her. "Let's move it." His urgency snapped at her.

"What did you do to him?"

"I made sure he didn't have access to any more weapons. He was talking to someone on his cell."

"Snyder?"

"I don't know. Maybe he called more of his buddies."

"Police?"

"Keep going, we have two more stories before we hit the ground. I smashed his phone, too. I idn't lay a finger on him, but he was cowering, olding his arm."

*Right. Because you already smashed his arm.* But she couldn't hold that against him. The man vas aiming to kill them.

On the ground, they hurried down the dimly it sidewalk. Cade tugged Leah to him and she vas grateful for the extra warmth. The memory f facing off with that man sent cold shivers all ver her. If Cade had reacted differently, or taken ven a millisecond longer to react, where would hey both be now?

"How did you know he wasn't the police?"

"I didn't." The gruffness in his voice scraped ver her.

"I thought the silencer gave him away," she aid. "That couldn't be legal."

"Might depend on what law-enforcement gency."

"What law-enforcement agency would have im shoot at us like that?" She stopped walking nd turned him to face her. "Cade. Are you tell-ng me you were prepared to run from the police f it came to facing them head-on?"

His tight expression said everything and noth-ng. "Call it instinct. I knew he would kill you.

Kill us. And that's not going to happen if I can help it."

Heat started in her stomach and spread around her heart, chipping away some of the cold. Breaking away at the part that didn't believe. That couldn't trust.

The magnitude of his willingness to sacrifice, especially after everything she'd dragged him into, slammed into her.

Shaking her head, she took off, walking fast. "I don't need you to do that for me."

Walking turned to jogging. Then to running. She fled from Cade. *He can't die for me. Can't die because of me.* As soon as she found the vehicle, she would leave him. It was the only way to keep him safe.

There.

Still parked in the alley, the vehicle Cade had rented waited in the shadows. For her. He was in this because of her. She ran, ignoring his call from behind. She knew that with his long legs he could catch her if he wanted to, but he gave her breathing room.

Leah made the car and leaned against it. Breathe. She had to breathe.

Cade clutched her shoulder.

"Come on, we're almost done with this. We have the map. Let's get what you need to put this man away and get your life back."

"I didn't get that list that would have told me the files Tim had checked out. I think that's the key here." But she knew there was no going back.

He unlocked the car and opened the door for her. She climbed inside. When Cade was seated, he started the ignition and turned up the heat.

She looked down at her trembling hands. Before this, nothing used to faze her. "You saved my life on that mountain. You saved my life tonight. I don't want you putting yourself between me and a killer again. Got it?"

"Got it."

His reply was out of character and surprised her. She hadn't expected him to agree. And it hurt. She hadn't expected that, either. Except that she didn't believe him. Not for one minute. He would, in fact, put himself between her and Snyder if it came to that. That was who Cade was. He had probably never told a lie until now. Until Leah. She had pushed him beyond his boundaries.

Cutting him free was for the best.

On the earliest morning flight to Juneau they could get, Cade couldn't help but notice that Leah had shut down. He didn't know if it was because of the kiss or the stress of being on someone's hit list, but she'd backed off from him, just when he thought he'd bridged the distance.

Exhausted from their night of cloak-and-dagger escapades, and surrounded by too many ears, they kept conversation to a minimum on the flight and didn't have a chance to go over their next step.

If it wasn't for the fact that she needed him to read the map depicted on the quartz, he had no doubt she'd disappear from his life. From a practical perspective, that might seem like a good thing, but pain zinged through him at the thought. He had no idea why he'd grown so attached to this woman.

Leah came with her own particular brand of problems. But Cade knew their time to figure this out, to uncover what her boss had hidden was about to end. Snyder was closing in. Taking more extreme measures. They had to elude him long enough to find the evidence of his crimes and then determine what this was all about. He hoped and prayed Leah could buy her freedom with what they would find with the map. Cade feared it would only bury her deeper, Cade along with her. But as he'd told her, he was in this for the long haul.

Once in Juneau, they hitched a boat ride back to Mountain Cove. Leah stood next to the rail on the boat, wrapped in her layers. Red with cold, her gloveless hands grasped the bar.

Cade took a risk and pressed his hand over

hers. "You should put on your gloves if you're going to stand out here."

She pulled her hand away and thrust it in the pocket of her fleece hoodie.

"We need to talk," he said. He had to get her to open up. "When we get back to Mountain Cove, let's go to the house for a bite, maybe a quick shower. Get cleaned up. Then we can grab the maps of the region I need back at the avalanche center to compare to the necklace."

Leah didn't respond.

"What's your problem?" he asked. "I'm already in the thick of this. No going back. Now let's finish it together. I know where to find whatever Tim hid. You need me. I promise not to take a bullet for you. I think that covers everything. Satisfied?"

A half grin slipped in to her lips. Pretty lips. Soft lips. He recalled the feel of them against his, pliable and responsive, and it toyed with his concentration. "I need to know what you're thinking," he said.

Leah looked over the side at the cold waters of the channel rushing beneath the boat.

"I don't know what I'd do without you," she finally said. "I would be dead twice over, and I don't want there to be a third time. I don't want you to get hurt because of me."

"Remember, Leah, I risk my life for others

on a weekly basis, if not daily, as a volunteer. I risk my life when I do field work for avalanche assessments. That can be dangerous, too. Don't think you're special." He injected a teasing tone. She was, in fact, very special to Cade, for reasons he hadn't figured out.

When she didn't respond, Cade watched the lush Tongass National Forest—the northernmost rainforest in the world—go by, looking as though it had seen days of rain on top of too much snow.

"Why do you do it, Cade? Rescue people? Risk your life for strangers?" Her blue-greens speared him, driving right through his heart with her question.

Where did he begin to answer that one? An icy breeze whipped over him and he jammed his hands into his pockets. "I don't know. It's a family thing, maybe. My dad served his community, served the people, for as long as I can remember until he died. Even then, he died saving someone." Cade paused. Swallowed against the thickness in his throat. "Dad...he was the best."

"You miss him, don't you?"

He nodded. "That's why I'd like to know what happened, you know? I'd like to know if Devon Hemphill set him up for that rescue. Set him up to die. And I can't know that until I know what they quarreled about, and even then, I still might not have the answers I want. Maybe those answers died with my dad and Devon."

"Then I showed up and brought the questions back to life." Leah looked away.

Maybe he'd been too harsh. But he'd been honest. "No matter how hard I work at my job, following in his footsteps at the avalanche center that he founded, or volunteering on the search and rescue team, I don't think I'll ever live up to the reputation my father had. Maybe that's why I work so hard, try so hard. I don't know. But I do know he deserved better than to die like that. He was a real hero."

She turned back to him then, pulled her hand from her pocket and thrust it inside his, wrapped her fingers around his, her foggy breath mingling with his own. "You are, too, Cade." Then her voice cracked a whisper, "You're my hero."

An invisible hand enfolded his heart and squeezed, lighting a fire in his chest. He'd do anything. *Anything* for this woman.

Not good. Not good at all.

Terrifying.

He would have done anything for Melissa. And she'd betrayed him.

# FOURTEEN

Back at home, Cade searched the house to make sure there were no intruders lying in wait. The house was empty, which was good on the one hand. On the other hand, Cade chafed at how empty it was without Grandma's cooking and affectionate chatter. Without Heidi who loved to rule and reign over him. He'd never have thought he'd miss the sibling banter. But he did. He missed them both. He'd done this to them.

The sooner this was over, the better. Then again, he wasn't sure how any of it would end. Would he or Leah, or both, be killed? And if they survived, what would keep Leah in his life when this was over?

One thing at a time. He tried to tell himself that he didn't want her in his life after this was over. But he knew that wasn't as true as he'd like it to be. He'd gotten this involved because he couldn't let her go after pulling her from the snow. But he'd had his fill of this situation, and he was sure she had, too.

He needed to clear his head before the next phase of this ordeal.

"Why don't you take a shower, clean up, if you want?" he asked. "I'll make us some sandwiches, then we'll head out to grab the maps."

She hesitated. "Okay, but…Cade, we need to hurry. I have a bad feeling. As though things could get any worse. I'm not sure it's a good idea for you to go further into this with me, I mean, after you tell me where to look."

He frowned. Was she crazy? She wouldn't find the destination without him, even after he showed her on the map. This thing could be buried twenty feet beneath the snow for all they knew. "We'll talk about that after sustenance."

Cade opened the fridge to pull out the sandwich fixings.

She rubbed her arms. "I'm not sure it's even a good idea for us to be here. What if Snyder shows up?"

He perused the inside of the fridge. "So far, he always shows up at night. It's only eleven in the morning. If he sticks to the schedule, we have a few hours." They were so close to ending this. He could feel it.

Exhaustion evident in the dark circles under her eyes, Leah nodded and disappeared up the stairs.

He didn't want to scare her, but she was right. Snyder could show up at any time. The man had to know things were coming to a close. He had to be more than desperate.

Cade placed his weapon on the counter. He hadn't told Leah of his plan to get Terry involved, thinking she would only buck and run if he told her. He understood her misgivings about trusting anyone, especially the police, given Snyder was a detective himself, but she couldn't know how well Cade knew Terry.

He grabbed his cell phone and made the call.

Pain erupted in his head. Everything went black.

Head pounding, Leah opened her eyes.

She scanned her surroundings— The cabin? What was going on? She tried to sit up, but that sent a sharp pain through her head. Leah blinked, grabbed her head and shoved herself upright.

Boots clunked, catching her attention. Snyder stood in a wide stance, staring at her. He sipped from a mug. Warmth blasted from a fire and the percolator sat on the wood stove.

Leah rubbed her eyes. She couldn't believe it.

"What's going on? What do you want from me?"

"Sorry about the headache. It will wear off. Not that it matters."

He didn't want to answer those questions? Fine, she had plenty of others to ask him. "Why did you kill Tim?"

*Are you going to kill me?*

He set the mug down, as if he had all the time in the world.

Oh, no. Cade. What happened to Cade? Leah stiffened. Skimmed the room for a weapon. An escape.

Snyder crouched in front of her. "I didn't want things to end this way. But your boss should have kept his nose out of my business. He made it his career to free criminals, just like you have, while I've given my life to put them away. But Levins just couldn't leave it alone. So I had to take extreme measures to keep criminals—the hardened ones, at least—from a life of crime."

"So that's your justification for becoming a criminal yourself?"

"I prefer to think of it as rendering justice when justice isn't served within the context of the law. You and your boss worked to free criminals."

Leah's mind swam back to what had happened to her mother. Why she'd become a legal investigator. "That's not true."

At least most of the time. Her mouth grew dry. What was he going to do with her?

Stupid question. Hadn't she known all along?

Where was Cade? Was he still alive? Would he save her? Mentally, she scolded herself for relying on another human being to help her.

Only God could save her. But would He this time?

"I'm going to ask you one more time to give me the information you and Tim uncovered." He tossed the shoebox on the floor in front of her feet. "Thought it was in that. You seemed to think it was so important when you were in his office."

"Wha—?" Her mouth hung open. "How did you know about that?"

He smirked. "Set up a surveillance camera in his office that feeds back to my phone. I'd just gotten back into Mountain Cove when I got a hit. Called Marlow to grab you, but wait until you exited Tim's office with the goods. But the idiot bungled it." Snyder unfolded himself from where he'd been crouched in front of her and tossed another log on the fire.

"And that's how you knew to find me at this cabin? The camera?"

He chuckled. "Nope. I came to the cabin hoping Tim had hidden what he was going to use to call attention to my activities here. I couldn't be sure you had witnessed anything, but even if you did, it would just be your word against mine. Then I found you at the cabin, which made my day. And I knew you either had what I was looking for, or you could find it for me."

He blew out a breath. "I'm glad this is over. I'm tired of making all these trips to Mountain Cove and to this sorry excuse for a cabin. Been looking at rental property on a nearby island while I'm here. Have to justify my reasons for coming, in case someone else digs around. But I'll have all the loose ends tied up after I'm done with you."

He turned his gaze on her. "So. Where is it?"

"I swear I don't know. Tim sent me on a long vacation. He never told me anything about you. I guess he didn't want me in the middle of this, but that's how it's going down anyway. He didn't involve me."

"You're his investigator. You're the one who dug this up!" Snyder tossed the shoebox in the fire.

"No!"

He snatched it back out and blew out the flames. "What's in here that's so important? What am I missing?"

"Nothing to do with you. It's for Cade." Now Cade might never get his answers.

"Isn't that sweet. You've fallen for your rescuer." Snyder chuckled. "I'm out of time here. If you can't tell me, or won't, and I can't find it, then nobody else will, either. I've already disposed of anything that might incriminate me that Tim had in his files and on his computer. Your computer is sorely missing anything pertinent, so maybe you're telling the truth. But as of this moment, you're the only loose end. You're the only witness."

"What…what are you going to do?"

"There's a warrant out for your arrest that hit the wires two hours ago, in case I'd lost you. I was tired of hunting you down. Here's how it goes. You and Tim were involved in a love triangle. Tim was cheating on you so you killed him. You wrote a suicide note. Then walked off into the mountains to die of exposure."

"You're crazy, you know that?" Panic strangled Leah; she wanted to jump from the sofa and tackle the man. "I'll never write that note."

"It's already taken care of." Snyder turned her laptop to face her. "I typed it up myself, and I'll send the email as soon as the deed is done. Then I'll give the cabin one more look around before I burn it down. I'm going to take you so far and so deep into the mountains, nobody will ever find you. See, Leah, I'm a dozen steps ahead of you."

"Listen to yourself, Snyder. You've become like the criminals you took upon yourself to judge."

"You're a barrier, standing in the way of justice. That's how I see it." He grabbed the percolator from the stove and poured more coffee. He held it up, looked at her. "Want one last cup?"

Leah shook her head, closed her eyes, hating that this man had gotten the best of her. She'd always thought she was so smart. So tough.

He must have killed Cade. That was why he wasn't here. The thought that he was dead because she'd taken refuge in his home, allowed herself to lean on someone, did her in. The will to fight seeped out of her. She slumped over on the couch, inhaling, exhaling shuddering breaths.

No!

Cade would want her to live. Would want her to fight until her last breath. Leah had her own brand of justice to render. She had to survive and make Snyder pay for his crimes. Make sure she found the evidence to put him away for a long time. Make sure that everyone knew he wasn't the hero he made himself out to be, but something dark and sinister.

Leah scrambled over the couch and lunged for the door. She'd rather face the brutal temperatures than wait for Snyder to mete out his own perverted form of justice.

His big hands gripped her, yanking her from the door. Pain shot through her arms, back and neck. Leah wasn't a screamer. She refused to scream. But Snyder ripped a scream from her all the same.

He covered her mouth, muting her cries for help. "What am I worried about?" He let his hand drop away. "Scream all you want," he said. "Nobody's going to hear you."

"Cade." The familiar voice broke through the darkness. "Cade, can you hear me?"

An ache ran through him. He squinted up to see Terry staring down in concern.

"Oh, thank You, God," Terry said. "I called an ambulance. Reed is searching the premises."

Cade sat up. "What happened?"

"That woman's what happened."

*Oh, no...*

"Leah?" Cade called, and tried to stand. Dizziness swept over him and Terry assisted him. "Where is she?"

"She's gone."

"Leah!" Feeling the knot at the back of his head, he stood, realizing he was in the basement.

His gaze landed on Terry who wore a knowing look. "She hit you over the head, dragged you down here and barricaded the door. You're fortunate your call to me connected before the line went dead. I came out here to see what was going on and found you down here."

Cade ran up the basement steps and made it to the kitchen before Terry caught up with him.

"Cade!" Terry grabbed him. Yanked him around. "Did you hear me? She's gone. She hit you in the head and left."

He thrust a sheet of paper in front of Cade. "See this? It's a warrant for her arrest. Did you know about this?"

"No, that's not right. She isn't guilty. She's been framed." Cade needed Terry to understand. To believe him. Leah had been right. They never should have come back to the house. Snyder was getting desperate. Cade had thought he'd be prepared to face the man if he showed up, but he'd failed again.

Utterly.

"That's what she told you?" Terry's demeanor made his skepticism clear. "Well, according to my sources, she's wanted for the murder of her boss, Tim Levins. Decided to do some checking on my own, and looks like I was just in time. She's been feeding you a pack of lies."

Head throbbing even more with the news, Cade shoved both hands through his hair and clutched the sides of his head. "No, Terry. Listen. Snyder must have her. He must have hit me on the head and taken her."

"Would you listen to yourself?" Terry paced the distance between the kitchen and the living room. "I don't want to think that one of my best friends has been assisting a fugitive, a murderer. Better to think that she fooled you. So tell me you didn't walk into this with your eyes wide open."

"She isn't a murderer."

An ambulance siren blared in the distance, getting closer. Emergency lights flashed outside the window. "No," Cade said. "No, no, no. I don't have time for this."

"Just where are you going?" Terry asked.

"I have to find her."

"You leave her to the law," Terry said. "That's our job. You're fortunate to be alive, Cade. Remember, she left you for dead in your basement. Now, I have to go out there and find her. But don't worry. She won't get far."

Terry opened the front door to let the EMTs inside. "I have to go to work. Once you have your head straight, I'll be back to take your statement. Do you get me, Cade?"

Cade nodded and watched Terry disappear. To the medic, he said, "I don't need you."

"Just let me check you over, and I'll decide if you need a trip to the hospital."

Shoving away, Cade headed for the stairs. "I promise I'll head to the hospital and get my head checked later. Right now, I have something else to do."

The man frowned, but he knew Cade well

enough to know he shouldn't bother arguing. "Suit yourself."

Cade made it up the steps and burst through the door to Leah's room. She'd packed all her stuff. Her laptop and her duffel were both gone. He dropped to the bed, holding his head in his hands. Was he an idiot, as Terry had made him sound?

Was it true that Leah had been the one to murder her boss, and Snyder was simply a detective using unconventional methods to capture a killer?

No. Cade knew exactly why Snyder wanted her. Cade had seen a man try to kill her with his own eyes. Even if Leah was guilty of something, there was more to all this, and she was in danger.

He popped a couple of ibuprofens and grabbed his Remington stainless 870 and his .44 Magnum. Cade slipped on his winter gear and grabbed his pack, already loaded down with his survival and rescue kit, radio and satellite phone and a pack with climbing equipment—just in case. With only a few hours of daylight left, this terrible day could turn into a long and hard night. In his truck, he started the ignition and headed out.

Whatever her boss had hidden was near Devon's cabin. Snyder might have taken her there. At least, that's where Cade would start his search. He drove like a maniac, praying all the way.

*God, please let me find her, save her.* God had intervened on Leah's behalf before, but He'd let Cade's father die. Cade had never understood why one person survived and another died, but as much as was within his power, he tried to keep people in the land of the living. He just had to hope God was on his side in this one.

If Terry wasn't going to listen to him—the only officer he felt he could trust with any of this—then Cade was on his own. Nobody was going to stand in his way. No way could he handle not being there again. He hadn't been there for Dad.

Heart pounding his ribs, he finally made the driveway up to Devon's cabin. He steered his truck over the road, bumping, swerving, sliding and plowing his way there. There were fresh tracks to the cabin. Leah?

Or Snyder with Leah?

Cade parked a short distance away, not wanting to alert Snyder if he was in the cabin with Leah. He grabbed his .44 Magnum and slipped from his truck, making quick time to the cabin. Smoke rose from the fireplace.

Bingo.

Sneaking around, he looked in every winlow, but no one was inside. Besides Leah's SUV parked in the makeshift garage, there wasn't an additional vehicle that Cade could see. His heart raced. Was she on her own in this, after all? Or had Snyder driven her vehicle?

He shoved through the door of the cabin to look around. Her laptop sat open on the table. Cade pressed a key and it came to life. He read an email she'd written.

Suicide? A confession of murder? Could any of it be true? No. This had to be part of Snyder's elaborate plan. In the distance, Cade heard the whine of a snowmobile. If Snyder had Leah, he was about to dump her in a place she would never be found. Within hours, another storm would be on them. Cade was running out of time.

He got hold of Isaiah on his satellite phone.

"Hey, bro, long time no hear. I have a quest—"

"Isaiah!" he interrupted, getting his friend's attention. "I don't have time. Listen to me. I need a big favor. It's a matter of life and death. I think Leah's been abducted. Can you fly over Dead Falls Canyon area around where Devon Hemphill's cabin is located, and see if you spot anyone? Relay back to me where I can find them."

"Sure. Adam and I'll go up. You want us to

contact the Alaska State Troopers? Get a search and rescue on this?"

Cade hesitated. Did he? No one was lost or injured yet. But someone had been kidnapped, he was sure of it. And if he was wrong? According to that email, Leah was planning suicide. But it would take a SAR team too much time to assemble. "Yes, but I'm going in on my own. There isn't time to wait. Will you do this for me?"

"Sure, but I can't be up there for long with the weather turning bad."

"I know. And, please, make it quick."

"Cade, be careful."

"I will."

Cade needed a snowmobile, too, and he didn't have time to go back down the mountain for one. He found some snowshoes, retrofitted and strapped them onto his boots. As soon as he got through the door, his spirits sagged. This was crazy. He would never make it in time. He wasn't a hero. He wasn't his father. He would never be the man Dad was.

He should call Terry to let him know what he was doing. That he thought Snyder had Leah up on the mountain. And if none of it was true, if Leah had pulled one over on Cade, then Terry could find her and arrest her.

Then he spotted it. A snow machine half

buried in the snow on Devon's property. Cade ogged in the snowshoes over to the machine and scraped the snow off. He had no confidence t would start, but not finding a key, hot-wired t anyway. It was as he had feared. The engine wouldn't turn over.

With a pleading heart, he glanced up at the heavy snow clouds.

*A little help here, please, God?*

His sat phone rang. "Cade," he answered.

"Spotted a man on a snowmobile, pulling a railer full of stuff," Isaiah said. "Couldn't see what. He had it covered up. But I didn't see anyone else with him."

"Where?"

"Headed up Mount McCann. North side. Lots of ledges and drop-offs there so it was kind of weird."

Cade's knees buckled at the news.

Snyder was looking for a place to dispose of Leah.

Had he already killed her?

"Thanks," he said. "Now get out before the storm hits. You know where I'll head if I can get there."

"You know the storm's expected to be harsh, dumping lots of snow. It's going to prevent any meaningful search and rescue. If you go, you'll be putting yourself in danger, risking your life You know that, right?" His concern breached the connection.

Closing his eyes, Cade blew out a breath "I know."

# FIFTEEN

Nausea roiled in Leah's stomach.

Snyder had duct-taped her wrists, ankles and finally her mouth because he was tired of listening to her. He hadn't killed her yet. Said he wanted the time of her death, in case she was found, to fit in the scenario he'd concocted. That would end any further investigation.

Beneath the hefty blanket, wedged between his winter camping gear, Leah rocked and rolled in the cargo trailer towed behind the snowmobile. She'd heard a helicopter in the distance, but she couldn't know if that was Cade searching or his avalanche team assessing the danger before the upcoming storm. She couldn't know if they had spotted a man pulling a trailer on a snowmobile—but even if they had, it was unlikely that that would raise any suspicion.

How could anyone reach her in time? She was responsible for her own rescue in this instance. She and God, if she could convince Him to intervene.

Leah guessed she had only a couple of hours if that, before Snyder shoved her off into som mountain gorge or crevasse in a glacier. He too a big risk himself, bringing her out here. Didn he remember the avalanche that had nearly kille them both? If he unintentionally drove over thin snow bridge, it could collapse and the would both die.

Whatever happened, he'd need to take car of her before it was dark and make camp if h couldn't make it back to burn the cabin befor the snow hit.

*God, is that all the time I have left?* She shu her eyes, panic engulfing her. She had sense all along that her time was running out, but sh had no idea what that had really meant. Was sh ready to die? In a spiritual sense, yes. She wa right with God.

In an utterly human survival mode sense? N way. No how.

*God, I know You're watching all this and tha You're with me. If there's any way I can get out c this, please show me what it is. And if not, pleas send help. Send Cade, because that would mea he's still alive. He doesn't even know what a rea hero he already is. The sacrifice he makes fo complete strangers. Please help him to see tha*

Leah's prayer turned to Cade and his family, and to her aunt who had raised her after her mother was incarcerated, and finally to Snyder, that God would open his eyes to the wrong he'd done. As her prayer ended on that selfless note, a sense of peace settled in her heart. No matter what happened, it was well with her soul, as the old hymn said.

The snowmobile stopped. This was it.

*Oh, God, oh, God, oh, God... Please, help me.* Leah hyperventilated.

The tarp came off first, then the blanket was ripped from her and a gust of icy air whipped over her. Snyder loomed in her vision. He lifted her as though she were nothing more than a sack of Idaho potatoes and set her on her feet in snow up to her knees. She fell forward, but he caught her. He threw her over his shoulder in a fireman's carry. Leah kicked and struggled.

"If you don't settle down, I'll have to knock you out now, and you won't get to look me in the eye before the end. You won't get any last words."

Leah stilled, a million scenarios of how this would end running through her mind. A million possible ways she could escape. But that was all insanity. There was no escape to be found.

Hopelessness seemed to reflect in the heavy gray clouds and warred with her will to fight.

Finally, Snyder set her to rest on top of packe[
snow, next to a pair of lone spruces at the edg[
of the tree line. He secured himself to the tre[
with a climbing rope, standing on the edge of [
jagged escarpment, as close as he could get with
out the risk of the snow collapsing beneath then
Hence, the rope. And there went her chance c
taking him with her.

He brandished a knife and held it to her throa[
"This is Suicide Ridge. Fitting, don't you think
I'm cutting you free, but any wrong moves an[
I'll have to end it with the knife."

The place looked more like a gash in the eart[
or a crevice than an actual ridge. Did he thin[
she would agree to make things easier for him
To help him fit her murder into a believable sui
cide scene?

He ripped off the tape, pulling hair with i[
Leah held her scream this time.

"Any last words?"

"Cade," she said, barely able to choke out th[
name. "He doesn't know anything. Leave hir[
and his family out of it."

"I'm impressed that you're thinking abou[
someone else instead of begging for your life
Warren is alive for now but don't think he'll ge
the chance to save you. Someone will have t[
find him first. I'm not going to kill him. I don[
need more collateral damage. He only know[

what you told him, which is hearsay. It'll just look like you duped him, lied to him. It would be his word against mine."

*Oh, thank You, God.* Cade would live. But if she'd learned anything about Cade in this short time she'd known him, the short time they'd had together—she knew the guilt that he hadn't saved her would eat at him every day.

Leah couldn't abide by that. She wouldn't fall down that ridge willingly. Snyder had the knife, so fighting against him was a risk, but one she was willing to take.

She'd been exposed to more violence at a young age than any child should ever have to see, and as an adult and a legal investigator, self-defense training had been a top priority. It hadn't worked so far in this situation, but it was all she had.

One more time…

Conscious of the knife he held, she took care not to telegraph her intentions. Dragging in a breath, giving him the impression she had one last thing to say, in one swift move, she lunged away from the knife and kicked him in the groin.

Wrong move.

They both tumbled over the ridge toward the icy abyss below, Leah reaching for something, anything to grab on to, her screams echoing into the deep darkness beneath her.

* * *

Adrenaline punching through him, Cad
gripped Leah's wrist with all his might, as sh
held on to the tree root thrusting out through th
soil layered in broken rock.

"I've got you!"

*Thank You, God...*

Terrified eyes stared back at him. Thoug
relief had infused Leah's face the instant he'
grabbed her, it was quickly dissipating. H
tugged her upward and grabbed her other glove
hand when she reached for him. "I've got you,
he said in that reassuring tone he'd learned t
use, even when he wasn't feeling it.

But the gloves were slipping. Lying prone, he'
had no time to anchor a snow picket to secur
himself. No time to grab a rope. He'd only ha
time to lunge and reach with everything in hir
as he'd come upon the scene just in time.

Hanging on his rope from below Leah, Snyde
stared up as Cade pulled her from the ridge. Sh
scrambled for traction on the snow-covered edg

Leah climbed over the ledge and hugged hin
For a moment he let her hold him tight, relishin
the feel of her safely in his arms, but finally h
eased her away. "I have to save Snyder."

"What? Are you crazy?"

"I can't climb, my arm got caught in the rocks,
Snyder called.

"I'll climb down and help you," Cade replied. The wind picked up, whipping around him.

He wasn't in a position to do a technical rescue from the rocky side of a ridge with an approaching storm. Nor could he expect any help that might be on the way to get here in time.

Pain pierced Cade's arm from Leah's fierce pinch. "He's a murderer. You're going to risk your life to save his?"

"She's the murderer," the man below yelled up. "Killed her boss, Tim Levins—my friend. I'm a police officer. I found her out here, trying to escape again."

"Right, that's why he dragged me out here to push me over the side."

He wanted to believe she was telling the truth, but what had Cade really seen besides the suicide email? He couldn't let himself dwell on that right now. The rescue needed his full focus.

Cade removed the equipment he'd need from his climbing pack and anchored his rope. All the while, Terry's words strangled him, keeping him from oxygen.

*She's wanted for the murder of her boss, Tim Levins.*

Leah grabbed him right before he descended, her eyes desperate, pleading. "You don't believe him, do you?"

His chest tight, Cade shoved back the images

of Melissa saying the same thing when he'd com
to rescue her and the man with whom she'd bee
cheating on Cade. The guy—Rob Garrison from
Juneau—proceeded to tell Cade all about how
Melissa loved him and not Cade. How she'd bee
spending time with him while Cade was work
ing.

"I don't know what to believe. But I have t
hurry," he growled. He could sort through thi
later. "A man could die if I don't act now."

"Cade," she pleaded.

He freed himself from her grasp. "This is wha
I'm trained to do. I'm prepared to risk my life
Leah, and yes, for a murderer, if it comes to that
It's not my place to stand in judgment like that.

But which one was the murderer?

Pain long and deep like the gash in the eart
he was lowering himself into flashed in her eyes

Maybe he was a sap, and would always b
a sap for pretty eyes. Maybe she'd killed he
boss—there was so much he didn't know abou
her.

"I'm coming. Hang in there," he called dow
to Snyder, hating his unintended pun. The ma
was more resilient than most, he'd give him tha

"Cade, be careful. You can't trust him. H
brought me here to kill me. To throw me over!

Cade glanced up but couldn't see Leah's face
"Stay away from the edge, it isn't stable."

Is this how his father had felt the last few min-
tes he was alive? When he risked his life for
 man he'd hated? Cade's father was worth a
 housand of Devon Hemphill. Cade squashed the
 noughts—he wasn't God and shouldn't think
 ke that. He wouldn't make that kind of judg-
 nent call. But even so, he hesitated rappelling
 ie ridge for a millisecond. Was he willing to
 isk his life for Snyder?

He stared down at the man who was clearly
 1 pain and who would die of exposure if Cade
 idn't do something. Of course, Cade couldn't
 :ave him stuck out there, facing the approach-
 1g storm head-on.

Cade descended the rocky face of the ridge,
 rateful that snow wasn't clinging to the rock, to
 ee what had snagged the man. Hoping he could
 elp him, he tried to shove aside Snyder's iden-
 ty. Tried to think of him as just another person
 Cade had to rescue. But as Snyder stared back,
 ttempting to project an innocent look and fail-
 1g, Cade recognized him as the same man who'd
 ollowed Leah in town. He'd know those dark
 nd devious eyes anywhere. The same man who
 ad claimed to be a witness at the avalanche.
 'his man had been stalking Leah to find out
 vhat she knew and then kill her. This guy was
 he guilty party, not Leah.

His gut twisted that he'd doubted Leah eve
for a second.

"What's going on?" Cade asked, eyeing Sny
der's arm.

"I was trying to get Leah. Trying to arrest h
when she shoved me over. When I fell I tried t
grab hold of something, only my wrist snagge
between the rocks and the harder I pull the mor
stuck I am."

Cade sensed the duplicity in him, in the wa
he projected a warm and friendly tone. It wa
all a lie. But Cade kept his thoughts to himsel
Confronting the man could wait until they wer
both on solid ground. For now, he pulled a picka
from his pack, thinking this could be a ruse o
Snyder's part to get Cade down here and inca
pacitate him. He'd never been in a position wher
he needed to consider the possibility.

"Let's hope I can chip some of the rock awa
and loosen your wrist. Then we'll see if you ca
climb up." He hoped so. He'd need more gear
Snyder couldn't make it up on his own.

Conscious of the heavy snow clouds, the droj
ping temperatures and wind gusts that pierce
like icy needles stabbing his face, Cade chippe
away at the rock that wedged Snyder's arm an
wrist. The gloves made the work clumsy, an
he hoped he didn't hit Snyder in the proces:

What would happen once the man was free? Cade tensed as he chipped more rock, ready for Snyder's reaction.

Ready to grab his weapon, already locked and loaded, if necessary.

*God, please don't let it come to that.* He didn't want to battle it out on the face of a ridge. Once Cade and Snyder made it back to the top, then Cade had no idea what would go down. But he did know that dusk would be falling much too soon, and with a storm almost on them, the three of them were about to get caught in something dangerous and deadly that had nothing at all to do with murder.

The rock fell away and, wincing, Snyder tugged his arm free. His coat was torn, and Cade noticed the blood.

"Thanks," Snyder said. "For believing me."

Snyder didn't actually think Cade believed him about Leah, did he? Cade stared the man down, acid crawling up his throat at the thought that he was helping this murderer get to safety.

"Not my place to decide if someone is worthy of being rescued. That's God's job." He ground his teeth, wanting to say more.

Snyder gave him a funny look.

"You going to be able to make it back up with

your arm?" Cade asked. "I can climb back an
pull you up." He hated this.

"I think I can make it. If not, we'll do it you
way."

Cade watched Snyder remove his gloves an
ascend the cold ridge as though he knew how t
climb, despite his wrist injury. And now, sud
denly, it was a race to the top.

This, Cade hadn't expected.

Fear snaked through his insides. He had t
make it up first. Had to reach Leah first. He'
counted on this man to cooperate with his res
cue so that he and Cade could both make it u
the ridge to safety. But what made Cade thin
he could trust the same guy who had been afte
Leah? The same guy who had murdered her boss

Breathing hard, Cade scaled the rocky clif
the sense of dread fueling him with adrenaline
Again images of his father with Devon flashe
in his mind. Had Devon killed his father ove
their dispute in a scenario like this one? Cad
reined in the deadly images bombarding him
He calmed his breathing. Focused on getting t
the top.

What would happen once they both made i
up? Cade thought through every possibility. Hi
weapon was ready to fire, tucked where he coul
reach it quickly.

He climbed over the ledge at the same time a

Snyder. As Snyder untied himself, Cade freed himself from the rope, never taking his eyes from the man, prepared to reach for his gun.

Tension crackled through the air, raising the hair on his arms and the back of his neck. Like two men in an Old West gunfight, the moment was now.

Cade yanked his loaded weapon out and aimed it point blank at Snyder, who had done the same. Cade now looked at the muzzle of Snyder's weapon dead on.

"Put down your weapon," Snyder said. "I'm a police detective, and you've been harboring a fugitive. This woman is a murderer and I intend to take her back to Washington."

"You're lying." The words spewed through Cade's seething lips. "You tried to kill her. You don't deserve the title 'detective.'"

Leah approached Snyder from behind. Cade wanted to warn her to be careful with words or his eyes, but he couldn't telegraph to Snyder that she was there. She hit his gun-wielding arm with a log.

Gunfire rang out. He'd gotten a shot off and barely missed Cade. Cade tackled Snyder, determined not to shoot him if he didn't have to.

He needed to subdue Snyder until help arrived. The man punched him in the face and Cade returned the favor. Wrestling in winter wear wasn't easy. Snyder shoved Cade into a spruce tree, forcing the air from his lungs. He grabbed Cade and knocked his already injured head into the trunk of the tree.

Blackness edged his vision. He struggled to see clearly.

Snyder was getting away. Leah tugged Cade behind the tree.

Another shot rang out. This one hit the tree next to Leah's head. Cade shoved her to the ground behind a large boulder.

"Here." She handed over the weapon Cade has lost in the scuffle.

Snyder shot at them again. Cade returned fire. They wouldn't survive the night shooting at each other. The winter storm would kill them first. "I need my pack."

He watched in horror as Snyder threw the pack containing food and survival gear over the ridge, then climbed on his snowmobile. Snyder fired two more rounds and they ducked behind the tree. Cade listened to the sound of the snowmobile starting up and heading off.

"Great."

Wind and snow whipped around Leah, her teeth chattering. "What do we do now?"

"We get out of this storm. Nobody can get to us tonight."

"You were expecting others?"

"Not really. Not with the storm. They know where I was headed and that I'll be okay until tomorrow. But I need my pack."

He hiked over to the ridge, leaning into the high-velocity winds the storm was handing out. "Why'd he have to toss my pack? My radio and satellite phone are in there, along with food and water and survival equipment."

"I think you have your answer." Leah wrapped her arms around herself, tucked her head. "He doesn't want us to survive. What are we going to do?"

"There's a trail shelter not far from here for hikers to stop and rest, or get out of the elements."

"But can't we hike down to the cabin?"

"It's too far. We'll never make it."

"And you don't think Snyder made for the same place?"

"Doubtful." Cade couldn't be sure of anything anymore except they had to get out of the weather. Unfortunately he was also certain that Snyder would be back for Leah, and now Cade. "Maybe he went back to the cabin, or maybe he has a camp already set up somewhere because he expected the storm. But let's find the shelter."

Cade grabbed the snowshoes he'd removed to descend the ridge and hiked over to the snowmobile he'd managed to get moving. "Oh, no," he said. "Those last two shots killed the snow mobile."

Leah's desperate gaze found his. "He left us to die of exposure."

# SIXTEEN

Even wrapped in her parka over several layers of clothing and her hood pulled tight around her head and over her mouth, Leah didn't feel as though she was wearing nearly enough. Her fingers and toes had grown numb. Leaning into forceful wind that pricked her face, Leah held on to Cade as he trekked through the snow. He wore one snowshoe and she wore the other one. It was the only way to keep from falling in snow that had grown too deep. With a chill that could steal her breath away and had already created tiny ice crystals on her eyebrows and lashes, this snowstorm terrified her even more than her experience in the avalanche had.

There was no choice except to focus with tunnel-like vision on Cade. No choice but to shove away the images of Snyder running up behind them and killing them both. Leah didn't doubt that he was crazy enough to take that chance in a blizzard.

"How much farther?" She yelled out the ques⸗
tion so Cade could hear her over the snow and
wind.

Glancing at her, his eyes peered through the
slits in his ski mask. He gave her a thumbs-up.
Whatever that meant. Then he turned back to
the task at hand—paying attention to the hike,
leaning into the storm and, hopefully, heading
to that shelter.

*Please, God, let the shelter be there. Lead
Cade in the right direction.*

Without it, they wouldn't survive the next
hour.

Cade turned on a flashlight they'd retrieved
from his climbing pack, which seemed useless
in the storm.

*God, thank You for saving my life back there.
For sending Cade. But I feel like I was rescued
from one calamity only to die in the next one.
don't want to be buried alive again, don't want
to die in this place.*

Snyder had meant to use the approaching win⸗
ter storm to his advantage—dump her with the
certainty that no one would find her body until
the spring thaw because this storm would bury
her deep.

Her legs sluggish, she tripped over her her⸗
self, falling to her knees in the snow, but Cade
never let go. He instantly turned and helped he

up. That he knew his way in this seemed impossible. Maybe he was secretly lost and was hiding that from Leah.

"You okay?"

She nodded, not wanting him to spend time worrying about her. But no, she wasn't okay. Leah trusted him to find their way. To a point. There were a thousand ways they could die tonight, the least of which was Snyder. Cade flashed the light up ahead. Leah peered through the trees that served as a small barrier from the pounding snowstorm. But she saw nothing.

Tension melted from Cade's grip. He practically ran, tugging Leah behind him. And then she spotted a small cabin—the trail shelter he'd mentioned. He pulled her up the steps and opened the door, tugging her inside. Cade shone the flashlight around the room and exposed a half cord of logs. "First order of business, start a fire." He shrugged out of his climbing pack, took off the one snowshoe and got busy making them a fire.

Leah wanted to make herself useful, but she was too cold to think straight. What was there to do until light and warmth filled the tiny cabin? What was there to do even when the fire was started? There was no stove to cook on. Nor did they have any food. But at least it was shelter from the storm.

In the meantime, Leah eyed the door, hoping, praying, that Snyder wouldn't burst through at any moment. She knew he wasn't done with them. Not by a long shot. He would stalk them and finish this before it was too late. Leah never dreamed anyone could be so tenacious, so driven. as though he would chase her to the ends of the earth.

She thanked God that Cade had showed up when he had back at the ridge. She wasn't sure how she felt about him saving not only Leah, but the man who was trying to silence her. Snyder had seemed almost as startled at the turn of events, but he'd disappeared to regroup.

Dim light and the crackle from the small fire caught her attention, filling the tiny room with warmth that had never felt so good. And hope. She stepped closer, wanting to shed her winter clothing, but she knew the room wasn't warm enough yet.

Cade turned to her, a grin on his face, but it couldn't cover the raw concern in his eyes.

"Come here." He reached for her. Pulled her to him and tucked her in his arms despite the bulk of their coats.

He was a pillar of safety and security. Leah closed her eyes and let herself lean on his strength. She'd never trusted anyone. Not with everything. But right now, what would it hurt to lean on him, if only for a moment? It wasn't as though she was giving away her heart. Her life.

Even though she wanted to do exactly that.

She'd meant to stay there in his arms for a mere minute or two. But she could have stayed there for an eternity and let all the fear drain from her. She might not be able to give her heart to Cade—not that he was asking—but she could trust him with her life. Deep down, she already knew that to be true.

He loosened his grip around her and stepped back. Positioned a chair near the fire. "Sit down and rest."

"What about you?"

"I'm good."

He pulled his gun out and set it on the small rectangular table that was shoved against the wall. Leah gestured with her chin. "Worried about bears?"

He arched a brow. "You could say that."

She blinked back unshed tears. "I didn't murder Tim."

"I know that."

"Back there. For a second. You doubted me."

"I've been lied to before. It was by a girl I loved." Cade busied himself with his pack. "You hungry?"

Letting the flames mesmerize her, she nodded.

"Here, catch." He tossed her a granola bar.

She caught it. "I thought you lost the food when Snyder tossed your other pack."

He grinned. "I forgot that I usually have bars stuffed in this for quick energy when climbing."

What had made him think he needed all this gear? He'd come prepared for anything.

She tore into the bar. "I don't blame you," she said.

"For what? Keeping energy bars handy?" After tugging off his coat, he positioned his pack and sat on the floor. His weapon stayed right next to him, pointed at the door.

"For doubting me…thinking that I could have murdered Tim."

"Oh." He stopped chewing.

"How can I blame you for that when I don't trust anyone myself? Distrust is second nature for me."

He leaned against the pack, the firelight making his face glow. The set of his rugged jaw and piercing gaze sometimes turned boyish. Like right now. Leah wanted to crawl onto his rudimentary pillow right next to him and snuggle. She wanted to trust.

To love.

The thought crushed her heart. She exhaled.

"Why is that?" he asked. "Why don't you trust people?"

That pensive gaze took over now, and he sat

up, watching her with more intensity than she could handle. She was glad she could stare at the fire. When this was all over and she and Cade parted ways, she would definitely feel his absence from her life.

A pang crawled over her heart. She wanted—no, needed—this nightmare to end. But she didn't want her time with Cade to be over. Why did the two have to be tied together?

She sucked in a breath. Did she want to answer his question? Tell him everything? That would reveal a big part of who she was.

No one knew her. Not really. Tim had known some of her story. Maybe that was part of the reason why he'd worked to keep her from becoming involved with investigating Snyder.

Leah decided the room had grown warm enough and shrugged out of her parka. She'd keep the hoodie on a little longer.

Cade reached over and covered her hand. "Hey. You don't have to tell me."

She squeezed back, not wanting to let go. To tell him, she'd have to think about a part of her life she wanted to forget. "No, it's okay."

He let her hand slip away.

"But if it's too hard to talk about…" He trailed off. Leah understood he was giving her an out.

She nodded. If there was anyone in this world she wanted to tell, it was this man. They could die in the next few hours or days, depending on the weather, depending on Snyder. If there was anyone in this world she wanted to allow herself to love and trust with everything she was, it was this man. He didn't have a traitorous bone in his body.

She sucked in a ragged breath.

"I was only nine. My mom worked at a diner. I never knew my dad, or even who he was. She always brought strange men home." Leah shuddered at the memory. "Some of them were nice, but most were no good. Unfortunately sometimes they would stick around for a while. Maybe two of them stuck around long enough to think of themselves as my stepdad. She'd send me to my room to play alone while she entertained her guy friends."

Leah risked a glance at Cade, hoping she wouldn't see pity. Please, no pity. But there in his eyes she only saw compassion and concern for her. He didn't say anything, but waited for her to finish. She wasn't sure she could.

"Don't get me wrong, she wasn't a prostitute. Nothing like that. She was just…lonely, I guess. She took good care of me. Fed me, clothed me and gave me shelter. And in spite of everything, I know she loved me. It was on one of those nights when I was sent to my room to play with my stuffed animals and old Barbie dolls. Someone pounded on the door loud enough to startle me. I heard loud voices. Two men arguing. I was scared. Scared for my mother. Scared for myself. I didn't know what else to do, so I crawled down the hall and hid behind a chair."

Leah pressed her face into her hands. "I saw… everything."

Tears threatened, but she sucked in another breath. She had to finish this. She had to tell someone. No one knew what she'd seen that night. At least no one who believed her. "My mother wasn't in the room. I didn't know then, but she'd gone to the corner store for cigarettes and beer. Her current boyfriend was facing off with another man. A stranger. I had never seen him before. Then my mother's boyfriend shot and killed that man and left. I didn't scream. I wanted to but I was too scared. So I sat there huddled in a ball. Frozen with fear."

"I'm so sorry, Leah." Cade's stricken voice broke through the images. "I don't know what to say."

She shook her head. "I'm not done yet. That isn't all of the story.

"My mother came back and found a strange man dead in her living room. She screamed and cried and shook me to find out what I had seen. I told her everything. But my mother didn't want me to tell anyone what I had seen. She was afraid for my life if the killer found out I'd witnessed his murder. Mom made something up about a burglar breaking in, but the police wouldn't believe her. The neighbors had told them plenty about her reputation, and they were convinced the murder victim was one of her boyfriends that she'd killed herself, during a fight. And even though I tried to tell them my story, they wouldn't listen. I was just a child.

"She was convicted of first-degree murder. My mother, an innocent person, was convicted and sentenced to prison...where she died."

Leah didn't say more, waiting for that to sink in. They listened to the crackling fire and wind howling outside the cabin.

"What happened to you?" Cade finally asked. "Where did you live then?"

"I went to live with my aunt and uncle. They offered me a better life than my mother had, but I was a troubled child after what I'd seen. If the police and the lawyers had been doing their jobs, if they had been concerned about justice in the first place, my mother would never have gone to prison."

The mesmerizing flames of the fire took her right back to that night, and Leah let herself relive it. Finally, she blew out a breath, spent. "So you see now why I became a legal investigator and went to work for a defense attorney. If there

s evidence out there to free an innocent person,
'm going to find it. So it seems beyond surreal
hat I witnessed another murder, and I could ei-
her lose my life for what I've seen, or be falsely
accused, like my mother."

The look on Cade's face nearly did her in.
No, it wasn't sympathy or pity, thankfully. Leah
never wanted that. It was something visceral. As
hough he understood her in a way she couldn't
even understand herself.

"I'm sorry you went through that," he said.
'You're the strongest person I've ever met. Now
I understand your determination to see this
hrough on your own terms. Why you've been
so unwilling to simply walk into a police sta-
ion and trust that they'd take your word over
Snyder's. You have good reason to mistrust the
egal system."

His admiration, and the somber grin that bled
into his face, snagged her heart and caught on
something deep inside. Leah wasn't sure how to
handle the feelings this man ignited in her.

When she glanced back up and caught him
studying her, she knew she had more to tell him.
This time it wasn't about her. It was about him.

"There's something else I need to tell you. I…
uh…"

Wow. This would be harder than she'd thought
it would be. She wasn't sure if this was the time

or if it was her place to tell him. But for the same reason she shared her story, she would give Cade the answers he needed. Then there would be no secrets between them—not on her part, anyway.

He sat up now, looking at the door. Had he heard something? What could he possibly hear over the storm?

He grabbed his gun and stood ready to shoot whoever entered. He motioned for her to get low and slowly approached the door. "Stay here," he whispered.

"No." She wanted to stop him. "You're not leaving me here alone while you go out there and get yourself killed."

Cade managed to don his coat while keeping his weapon trained on the door. Finally he opened it, letting in a gust of wind and snow that rushed through the cabin, whipping around the fire and nearly blowing it out.

Then Cade disappeared.

With his back to the cabin, he walked the perimeter, gazing into the darkness, holding off shining the flashlight. He wasn't sure what he thought he'd heard, but he couldn't take any chances.

All his experience and various SAR training hadn't prepared him for what he would face when he'd pulled Leah from the snow that day.

Hadn't prepared him to face off with a trained killer—an officer of the law, no less.

He couldn't see a thing, but instead listened, trying to hear anything unusual inside the storm.

Something cracked to his right. Cade pointed his weapon, unwilling to shoot until he could see what or whom he was shooting at. "Show yourself or I'll shoot."

Stupid. As if Snyder would answer that. If it was even him. How could the man have stalked them so effectively in this storm? He must have set up camp using an extreme weather tent and gear. But what kind of crazy would you have to be to do it in this weather? Regardless, the temperature had dropped severely, and Cade wouldn't stay out much longer. Whoever was out there was insane.

But then, he already knew the detective had gotten twisted somewhere along the way. He'd turned his back on the law he'd sworn to uphold without even realizing who or what he had become.

With the storm raging around him, Cade decided that he had become the crazy one. His paranoia was making him hear things. Snyder couldn't have followed them to the cabin. Not in this storm.

He turned to go back inside.

An arm wrapped around his throat.

Cade tugged at the strong grip, his need to breathe and keep the man from crushing his trachea warring with his ability to fire his handgun.

Darkness edged his vision. But he couldn't free himself.

And if he didn't? Not only would Cade die, but Leah would, too.

It was now or never. Cade aimed and fired his weapon into the ground.

Snyder's grip loosened, accompanied by a shriek. Gasping for breath, Cade whirled to face the man. But he limped off into the darkness, likely leaving a trail of blood behind him. Cade aimed his gun, struggling not to shoot. He wanted to fire at him. But he couldn't shoot a man in the back. Not even a killer.

And Cade wouldn't go after him in this.

Leah ran outside, screaming. "Cade!"

He turned, grabbed her and pulled her back inside. Leaning against the door he soaked in the warmth, let it heat his chilled bones, his frozen cheeks. He had to stop facing off with the man this way. He was running out of ammo.

"Cade." Leah held his frozen hands between hers to warm them. "What happened out there? I can't believe you saw Snyder. How could he—?"

Cade shoved from the door. "He has to have a base camp set up somewhere nearby. The guy's a mountain climber and knows how to survive out here, too. That much is obvious. It's also clear that we're not safe here."

"But we don't have anywhere else to go in the storm. If we can't move, then he can't, either."

"If the storm lets up he'll be back."

Drained, he plopped in the chair and held tight to the handgun. *God, what do I do? How do I protect Leah?* A lifetime of saving and rescuing and protecting people flashed through his mind. First, his hero father and now him… What was it all for, if in the end he couldn't save himself, couldn't save the woman he loved?

He glanced up and caught her watching. He wished he could take her in his arms. Tell her everything would be okay.

"A team will be out looking for us first thing in the morning when the storm moves through. Isaiah will find us. He'll take the helicopter out. He knows where to look."

Leah's gaze held his, searching. He'd always put so much effort into reassuring people that everything was going to be okay. Though he'd given Leah his best, he knew his words had fallen flat. A rescue team arriving in the morning might be too late to save them. But he'd give his best, his all, do everything he could tonight. He would stay awake and watch. Protect Leah.

"Cade, before you went outside, I was going

to tell you something. I want to tell you now, before it's too late."

*Before it's too late*. In case the worst happened, she meant. She didn't voice it, and he wouldn't, either.

She had his attention. "Go on."

"It's about the cabin. The box I found in Tim's office contained letters and receipts and slips of papers."

He stiffened. "What did you find?"

"You wanted to know about the quarrel your father had with Devon."

A knot grew in his bruised throat. "I still do."

"Remember, it's my job to look at the evidence, to figure things out."

"I have a feeling I'm not going to like this."

She looked at her hands. "I'm not sure I'd even be telling you this if it wasn't for the situation we're in."

He wished he didn't understand what she meant about not leaving things unsaid before it was too late. He'd always live with the regret of the argument he'd had with his father the day he was killed. Those last words between them would always be there, hovering in Cade's conscience. Gone unsaid were the things he *should* have told his father—that he'd loved and admired him and always would.

"I hope you're not upset that I looked through

ie box. But Tim believed the cabin should have
one to Devon's daughter and had asked me to
ok into this woman's disappearance. So, in a
wisted sort of way, considering Tim is dead, I
iought it was part of my job as an investigator.
.nd to be honest, I was hoping to find something
> help you. That's why I looked through the box
n the ferry back to Mountain Cove."

"Tell me."

"Your father." Her eyes raised to meet his gaze
nd pinned him. "He had an affair with Devon
lemphill's daughter, Regina. It was years ago,
ke twenty or something. There's a few letters
ack and forth. But from what I could gather in
ie letters, Regina got pregnant. She left Moun-
iin Cove when your father ended things be-
veen them because your mother was sick."

# SEVENTEEN

Cade had no problem staying awake, given th
news that Leah dumped in his lap.

It was all he could do not to call her a liar. F
wanted it to be a lie, but Leah claimed there wer
letters between the two. Evidence such as th
was hard to ignore. What he wouldn't give to g
his hands on those letters. But if Snyder torche
the cabin, the box and letters and Cade's answe
would go up in flames along with it.

All he could do now was trust Leah. Sl
looked into things like this for a living, so l
had no excuse not to take her assessment fe
God's truth.

He leaned his head against the logs, watchir
the door, holding the handgun he'd reloaded wi
the last six bullets, while she slept in front of tl
fire, wrapped in her coat. The storm had blow
through, and Cade heard nothing but the dee
quiet that came after a blustering snowstorm.

If he heard the snap of a twig, or the crunch
f footfalls in the snow, he'd know.

He would be ready.

But his mind and heart tripped over thoughts
f his father cheating on his mother. Anguish
ngulfed him. All these years he'd spent look-
ng up to the man. All these years he'd tried to
e the hero his dad was, the man his dad would
ant him to be. He wanted nothing more in this
orld than to live up to his father's reputation,
nd Cade always failed. Or at least he'd thought.

But to hear that his father was an adulterer?
hat he'd lied and cheated on his wife and fam-
y? Cade struggled to wrap his mind and heart
round it even as he drowned in disappointment,
eep and cavernous.

And to think, if the pregnancy had gone to
rm, he had a half brother or sister out there
omewhere…

*Whop-whop-whop.*

The distant sound of a helicopter jolted Cade
wake. Ignoring the crick in his neck from sleep-
ng in an awkward position, he shoved to his feet,
ngry at himself for falling asleep in the first
lace. Some protector he was—Snyder could
ave walked in on them. From where she lay

next to the fire, Leah stirred in the cold cabin the warmth from the embers nearly gone.

Her eyes grew wide when she recognized th sound.

She jumped to her feet and put on her coa same as Cade. Then she rushed to the door.

Cade blocked her way. "We need to be car ful."

"We need to let them know where we are Leah tried to move by him. "That we're her and alive."

"That, too, but Isaiah knows I would hav come to this cabin. A rescue team won't be fa behind. But I'm going out first. Got it?"

Cade opened the door to a wall of snow, up t his chest. "Just what I thought."

He used the pickax from his pack to dig an clear enough of a path so he could climb ou Then he put on both snowshoes. Leah could sta here while he let the rescuers know where the were.

Gunfire echoed outside, the sound splinterin through the timber of the rudimentary trail she ter and thundering through Cade's chest.

Leah stood frozen as another shot rang out.

The helicopter's rhythmic vibration of roto shifted and slowed, and the engine gave a hig itched whine. Something wasn't right. She saw nger and panic slice across Cade's face.

Standing in the doorway, he looked back at her. "Stay here." He ground out the words.

She knew he was afraid of what had happened. Afraid of what was *about* to happen. Most likely, he feared for his friend, if Isaiah was in that helicopter.

"But what if Snyder comes and you're not here? I don't have a weapon. No way to defend myself."

He shook his head as though shaking off a veil of confusion and crawled over the snow and out the door. This cold nightmare was getting to them both. She followed.

"Stay close." Cade tromped quickly across the snow, leaving Leah behind.

Without snowshoes, she couldn't keep up and tumbled as she waded through hip-high snow, deeper in some places, pushing through and taking big steps. Breathless, she leaned against a tree, packing the white stuff down, fearing she would fall in a spot over her head and be lost forever.

A clearing up ahead caught her attention. Cade headed that way. Had Isaiah been trying to land?

But then she saw it all.

Time seemed to stand still. Cade stood fifty

yards ahead of her. The helicopter was spinning out of control, not far from the ground.

And then.

Just like that.

It crashed.

Heart pounding, Leah caught up to Cade. He ducked behind a tree and pulled her with him, his chest rising and falling with his heavy breathing.

"Oh, Cade. Was that Isaiah?"

He turned her to face him, gripping her arms, sorrow and anger flashing in his eyes. "The snow was deep enough, he survived. He had to."

"What happened?" Leah couldn't believe any of this was happening.

"Snyder's still out there."

"Are you saying he did this? How?"

"Shot out the tail rotor probably."

"Why? Why would he shoot down a helicopter?"

"That was your only way out, away from him. Our only way out. He knows he has run out of time. He has to get rid of us now before the others get here." He tucked her behind him and fired his handgun. "He's in the trees. I have to get to Isaiah. See that? That's a snow cornice. We need to stay out of the path in case it collapses. It could trigger an even larger snowslide."

Avalanche.

A knot grew in Leah's throat.

"We'll make a run for it." He gripped her arm. "Keep low. Stay behind the trees."

Before Leah could react, Cade fired a shot off into the trees across the clearing. She could have used some warning. Her ears were ringing now. Cade ran to another copse of trees, tugging Leah behind him. When they reached the trees near where the helicopter went down, the dead silence made her heart sink. How could Isaiah have survived like Cade said? Of course, she knew he'd said the words to convince himself.

Cade looked at the Magnum. Made sure there wasn't any snow in the bore. Then he handed her his weapon, grip first. Leah took hold of the massive handgun. It was much heavier than hers. Why was he giving it to her?

"You cover for me. I'm going to pull Isaiah out."

Wait. What? "No, Cade. I can't do this. I can't be responsible for your lives." Any more than she already was.

"You can do this. You have to cover me."

He wrapped his gloved hand around hers on the grip. "Be careful you don't hurt yourself. It has a big recoil. It has a heavier trigger pull than you're probably used to so keep that in mind. And there are only four bullets left. Make them count."

Leah pleaded with her eyes.

"I have to go," he said. "You can do it. There'[s]
no other way."

Knowing he was right, she nodded. She dragge[d]
in an icy breath, then peered from behind th[e]
tree. Snyder was moving, but when he saw Cad[e]
heading toward the helicopter, he aimed hi[s]
weapon. Leah fired a shot off, the blast knock[-]
ing her on her backside. What she wouldn't giv[e]
to have her own weapon right now. She crawle[d]
forward and looked for Snyder. He'd ducked be[-]
hind a snowbank, out of sight.

Cade ran from the protection of the trees fo[r]
the downed helicopter.

Leah's hands trembled, something she couldn'[t]
afford. Now there were only three bullets left[.]
This wasn't going to work. She couldn't hol[d]
Snyder off with only three shots.

She watched for movement from the snowban[k]
or in the trees across the clearing on the othe[r]
side. Nothing.

And then Snyder was making his move again[.]
He hiked down and away from the helicopter[,]
crossing the clearing toward Leah. She fired a[t]
him, and he ducked again.

Two bullets left.

A glance at the helicopter showed her Cad[e]
assisting Isaiah out. He was alive. When Sny[-]
der took aim at Isaiah and Cade, Leah shot a[t]
him again.

He ducked and she missed.

She only had one bullet left and had to make t count.

As Snyder made his way toward her, both Isa-ah and Cade were also in the line of fire—in Snyder's sights. This was all her fault. And it was up to her to resolve it. Cade hadn't meant or Leah to shoot to kill. But that's exactly what Leah intended to do if Snyder took aim again.

Leah ducked behind trees and headed toward Snyder this time. Tired of being on the run, being on the defensive.

This time she was on the offense. This detec-ive sworn to serve and protect wouldn't take lown another person to cover his crimes if Leah ad anything to do with it. She'd tried to find he evidence she needed to put him away—and t was still out there, waiting to be dug up—but he was here.

Now. Facing off with a killer.

She'd never killed another human being. Couldn't imagine what that felt like. Didn't want o know. She'd seen enough bloodshed to last a ifetime.

Footfalls crunched in the snow behind her. Cade and a limping Isaiah.

Ducking from tree to tree, Leah continued naking her way to Snyder. The boldness grew

inside her as she prepared to face him one las
time. To end this.

With one bullet left, she intended to mak
it count, as Cade had said. For his and Isaiah'
sake, if not for her own.

"Leah!" Cade said loud enough for her to hea
him from behind. Hopefully not loud enoug
for Snyder.

But Cade was too far behind. He wouldn'
catch her.

Leah spotted Snyder again. What was h
doing? He moved and acted as though he'd los
sight of Leah, which meant she had the advan
tage.

Watching, waiting, Leah hid behind the tre
until she saw him trudging in the opposite direc
tion. To the trees across the clearing. Why wa
he running? What had him scared?

*Oh, no, you don't.* She didn't plan to live an
other day in fear that he would find her.

"Snyder!" she called.

Leah followed him across the clearing, stum
bling. Almost falling face forward.

Then Snyder turned to face her.

There was something eerily familiar about thi
scene. About this moment. Then she realized
They'd faced off just like this before—when he'
first tracked her down. They'd both nearly die
then. Would they die today?

# EIGHTEEN

Snyder lifted his weapon and aimed at Leah.

Leah aimed at Snyder.

Cade couldn't believe his eyes. This could not end well. She had one bullet left, if he'd counted her shots right. But Cade had Isaiah's gun now and ran toward her.

"No!" Cade aimed and fired.

Snyder dropped before he could get off a shot. Then Leah dropped to her knees. Was she hurt?

But Cade had no time to think about that. Prickles ran over his skin. Dread churned in his gut. Three thoughts went through his mind at the same time. Snowstorm. Cornice. Danger. He looked to the crest of the mountain at the exact moment the cornice collapsed.

Blasting snow rumbled toward them.

Cade, Isaiah, Leah and Snyder. They were all in the path.

Terror gripped Cade.

He was an avalanche specialist. This shouldn't

happen to him. Shouldn't happen to his friend under his watch.

Shouldn't have happened to his father, an expert, while out on a rescue.

But he understood now. Knowing the imminent danger didn't keep him from being pulled into this nightmare.

Cade's world.

Tipped.

Over.

Leah stood and whirled around in slow motion to look at him one last time.

Isaiah grabbed Cade, tugging him to run to the side and out of the path of the avalanche. But Cade pulled in the opposite direction to save Leah.

No way would she make it to safety. No way could Cade leave her there to go through it alone. He'd told her he would never leave her.

"Leah!"

The panic and fear written on her features cut through him like nothing before, but her eyes told him to save himself. Her demeanor said she was resigned to her fate.

"No!" He ran to her, reached for her.

Then the world collapsed in a wicked, fast-moving river of snow.

Cade tumbled in the crushing torrent, wild terror pulsing through him. For the first time he felt completely out of control. He could do nothing to save himself.

Nothing to save the others caught in the slide. Nothing...except...

Surrender.

Leah had been right all along. Cade couldn't control everything. Couldn't save everyone. Couldn't even save himself this time.

Though his terrified prayer was feeble—God was all he had in this moment.

*Save...us...*

In that instant the river of snow and ice stopped.

He calmed his breathing. He wasn't dead from impact with a tree or debris. Had made it this far.

*God, help Leah and Isaiah. If You have to take someone, take me.* Silence wrapped around him like the answer he expected.

*You saved her once. I can't believe You'd save her to let her die in another avalanche.*

Cade waited in the silence and the cold, hoping he wouldn't run out of air. Hope played with him. Toyed with his heart and soul. Hope that the search and rescue team that was already on its way would make it in time. Had even witnessed the avalanche. Would pull them all out.

But what were the chances?

Icy cold crept in, chilling his bones and his heart. He'd been involved in enough rescues that

he knew their chances of survival were close
to zero.

*Why, God? Why?*

Is this how his father had felt? Had he lived
long enough to die alone? Or had he died instantly?

Then he heard it. The smallest of sounds
muted by the crushed snow entombing his body.
Voices.

Voices!

*God, let them find Isaiah and Leah.* And, yeah,
maybe Snyder, too. If he survived, he should face
justice for his crimes. Cade had his beacon on.
Always had his beacon on. But Snyder had intended for Leah never to be found, so she didn't
have a beacon. There could be no doubt there.

Cade—idiot that he was—he should have
made sure she'd worn one. He should have given
her his.

They'd found him. Were digging him out now.
But he wanted to die. How could they find Leah
in time?

He hadn't been buried far from the surface and in no time, he looked into his brother
David's relieved face. With help, he scrambled
out of his tomb.

"You okay?"

"Leah. Where is she? Have you found her

yet?" Cade searched the area where rescuers were digging for one person.

"We found another beacon."

"Isaiah." Had to be, by the trajectory.

Cade searched the area in front of him, concentrating on where he'd last seen Leah. "Leah!" he called, knowing she wouldn't answer.

"Dig! David, get searchers with poles over there." He pointed.

"Calm down." David grabbed him. "We'll find her."

Cade had said those words, those lies, enough times himself to know they had little hope of getting her out alive. The only saving grace was that the team was here and onsite almost immediately after the avalanche stopped.

But a fierce nausea roiled in his stomach and Cade wanted to drop to his knees. To give in to it. But he couldn't do that. Not now.

Not with a life at stake. Leah's life. How could he be in this position? Saving her again? *God, please let us save her!*

A second team arrived. David and Cade instructed them where to search, and Isaiah— freshly released from the snow—joined Cade. Cade grabbed him in a bear hug, glad his friend was okay, though he'd need to get his leg checked after the helicopter crash.

Heidi appeared and hugged Cade briefly.

She and Isaiah looked at each other for the longest time, then she grabbed him, holding him close.

"Found something," another rescuer called.

Cade made his way over and started shoveling and digging for all he was worth. Leah's life depended on it. Then, slowly, he saw something in the snow.

It was a black ski parka.

For the second time nausea roiled in Cade's stomach. This wasn't Leah. This was Snyder. He stepped back to let someone else dig. Not protocol, but he had to find Leah.

"This isn't her. Come on people."

Desperate, he scanned the debris field. *God, why? Why did we find this murderer instead of Leah?* Cade had shot at Snyder to injure him, to bring him down before he killed Leah. But he hadn't fired to kill him. So he could be alive even now.

"Over here," a rescuer called closer to the tree line.

*Oh, God, no.* If she'd been pushed into the trees…

And even if she'd escaped injury from the trees, they were looking at twenty minutes now, going on half an hour. He'd only thought he'd been out of control when the snow slide rushed over him. His inability to find the woman he loved crushed the breath inside from him. This moment would destroy him.

That is, if they didn't find her alive.

Cade was there, digging faster than anyone, his love driving him on. Hope and terror forcing the snow out of his way.

And then…there she was. Her beautiful face. Eyes closed; there was an expression of peaceful serenity captured on her features.

This time she didn't look back with relief in her vivid blue-green gaze, pleading with him to get her out. She stayed perfectly still. Cade staggered back, his heart splitting open.

"Keep digging." He dropped to his knees to work to free her.

Usually they would check for a pulse first, then proceed. But Cade would have none of that.

They pulled Leah out and laid her on the snow. "She's gone," someone said.

"No. Don't even say that." Cade's sharp tone cut through the tension. He couldn't believe she was gone. He wouldn't accept that. "See if you can find her injuries while I do CPR."

Cade immediately began compressions. Leah wasn't dead. He wouldn't allow it. All the frustration of losing his father rolled over him. He should have saved his father. He needed to be in control again, but all the control he thought he'd had over his life, or tried to have over his life and the ones he loved, had been a joke. He'd never once been in control. He could accept that, accept that it was in God's hands. But that didn't mean he couldn't try to do his part.

What use was being a hero if you couldn't save the people you loved?

"Come on, baby," he said between compressions. "Come on. You are not dying on me."

"Cade, she's gone, man." David's voice stabbed Cade.

He was required to keep doing CPR until the medical personnel arrived, anyway, so David could keep his mouth shut. Regardless, Cade would do this until Leah came back to him.

"She could have brain damage," someone whispered behind him.

He gritted his teeth. "No. She had an air pocket. She'll be fine."

Cade gripped her shoulders and shouted into her face. "I love you, Leah. Don't leave me."

Leah sucked in a breath.

Her eyes fluttered open.

She dragged in a cold breath.

Cade's face filled her vision. Were those tears streaming from his eyes? Her heart leaped at the sight.

Cade had made it. He was alive. And she was, too.

He cracked a grin. "You scared me half to death."

"And you saved me again."

"Ma'am, can you tell me if you're hurt?" another man asked. He wrapped a blanket around her.

Leah shook her head. She didn't know. Didn't care. All she cared about right now was the love she saw streaming from Cade's eyes. She moved to sit upright. She felt a little dizzy maybe, but she didn't care. "Help me up."

A man approached as Cade helped her to her feet. She recognized him as Cade's police officer friend, Terry. "Detective Snyder is dead."

That should have been the most important thing to Leah. Relief that she would no longer be stalked by this murderous maniac. She wondered if it had been Cade's bullet that had killed him or the avalanche. But she couldn't keep her thoughts on that when the only person who mattered was the man in front of her.

"Thank you," she whispered.

"It's my job." He gave a teasing but shaky grin.

"You did more than your job. You rescued me from that killer." Leah reached up to touch Cade's cheek but hesitated.

"Why?" Now she felt her own tears sliding hot down her cheeks. She wanted to know if what she'd heard a few moments ago was true. "Why would you go that far? And don't tell me it's because of your job."

Was she reaching here? Asking for something she wasn't entitled to? Making a fool of herself?

Leah realized at that moment that the others had left them alone. They'd probably understood that she and Cade needed privacy. Cade stared at her as if he didn't want to let her out of his sight.

"I heard something," she said. "I thought I heard you say something."

He smiled then. Would she ever grow tired of that grin?

"I think my exact words were 'I love you, Leah. Don't leave me.'"

"I heard right, then."

"You heard right. What is your response to that?" he asked.

"I'm not going anywhere."

Cade *loved* her? Since losing her mother she'd never gotten close enough to anyone to let them love her. Or to love them back. And yes, she loved him back. At that moment her love for Cade overwhelmed her, in fact. Someone she could trust with her life and her heart stood right in front of her. She'd never intended to give so much away.

But, for the first time, Leah had found someone worthy of that risk. Cade was worth risking everything for, and maybe, just maybe, that was because he'd risked everything for her first.

Cade pulled her near, leaned in and kissed her, long and hard, until she was breathless. Warmth spread from her face down through her body, chasing away the numbing cold. He wrapped his arms around her, pulling her good and tight, in spite of their coats, and deepened his kiss, as though they weren't surrounded by rescue workers.

Suddenly nothing else mattered. Not the avalanche or her near-death experience. Not Snyder's attempt to kill her. Not the mountain or rescue workers. Only Cade mattered now. How had she found someone like him to love her, when she hadn't even been looking? When Cade eased away slightly, disappointment surged. Leah didn't want this to ever end.

He pressed his forehead against hers. "I thought I'd lost you today. And, Leah, I don't ever want to lose you, if that's okay with you." Cade tugged her a little closer. "Let's get you out of this cold."

He ushered her to the medevac where they were assisting Isaiah with his injured leg.

Leah sat in the helicopter, Cade next to her. This was déjà vu. She still hadn't given him an answer, at least not the answer she knew he wanted, but there was too much going on around them.

Back at Cade's house, Leah sat next to her duffel bag on the bed. Her things had been retrieved from the cabin, but the authorities had retained her laptop for evidence, since Snyder had typed a suicide email for someone to find after he killed her.

It was hard to believe he was gone. But she wasn't sure this was over. She'd always suspected he couldn't work this alone—a suspicion proved by the man who had attacked them at the law office. There had to be others backing him, supporting him when he killed criminals that Tim had gotten off. And she'd held on to the necklace with the map. She hadn't handed that over yet.

She tugged it from where it hung beneath her sweater, surprised Snyder hadn't paid more attention to it. They needed to dig up whatever Tim had hidden, and she hoped it would include the evidence against any other guilty parties, as well.

She was still scared. Sure, the police were in on everything now and seemed to believe her story. Internal Affairs would be swarming soon. They would arrest Marlow—the man who'd tried to detain them at Tim's office—but someone else could be scrambling to get away out there. They might want to dig up Tim's evidence, too, so they could destroy it forever. Or maybe they would want to silence the only witness to Tim's murder. The only person who'd discovered what was going on. Cade couldn't be counted as a witness in that regard.

He knocked on the doorjamb and leaned against it. "Hey."

"Hey." The word felt unnatural. Uncomfortable. Where did they go from here?

He'd told her he loved her. Leah hadn't said the words back to him yet.

He stepped into the room. "Terry needs the necklace. We're going for the evidence now. I trust him, Leah. He'll make sure the wrong people don't get their hands on it and destroy it, okay?"

She hung her head. "Okay."

Standing in front of her, he tugged her to her feet and slid his hands over her shoulders, around her neck and through her hair, cupping her head. Cade kissed her again, and she kissed him back. She'd never wanted anything or anyone more. They could take care of each other. That is, if Leah would only let herself be with him.

Cade eased away, and sighed. Clearly he was as concerned about what happened next as she was. "I never wanted to love anyone again. I actually thought I was immune to it, after the pain I'd gone through. I believed I'd never trust someone enough to love. But then I pulled you from the snow and nothing has been the same since." His tone was calming and reassuring, as it had been that first time he'd dug her out of an avalanche.

But she also heard a desperation there she'd never heard before. Cade Warren was scared to death that she was going to hurt him. She understood what it had taken for him to love her, and for him to lay it all out there. She could tromp right over his heart. But he'd taken that risk with her.

She gazed into his intense eyes, remembering that first moment she'd looked into them. She'd never met anyone whose eyes conveyed so much emotion. So much passion. Leah might exist, but she couldn't hope to really live without this man in her life.

But he was the one to voice the words. "Life isn't worth living. Saving people has no meaning if I don't have someone that I love by my side."

Leah went into his arms, hoping and praying she could always feel this way, safe and secure in the arms of a hero.

# EPILOGUE

Six weeks later Cade and Terry made another attempt to find the evidence Leah's boss had supposedly hidden. The weather had dumped more snow than they'd seen in years, preventing them from successfully digging up the buried evidence, though two police departments and Internal Affairs needed it. Cade wasn't sure how Tim had managed to bury anything, but if they had gotten the coordinates on the map correct, this was the spot.

Leah hung back and watched. She'd returned to Kincaid to assist in closing Tim's office and to pack up her apartment so she could move to Mountain Cove. She'd found a job with a local attorney, a friend of Terry's. She and Cade both needed to see where their relationship would lead them.

But Cade knew. He'd known from the first, though he'd tried to ignore the truth. Now he waited on her to realize they were meant to be together.

Until this was all behind them, Leah wouldn't be ready for anything from Cade. So to that end, Cade was determined to dig up the treasure, so to speak, and hope it was worth all the trouble.

The police had not been able to detain Marlow, the police officer who had worked with Snyder, after all. He had disappeared, which left them to believe he had gone into hiding. Leah might always have to look over her shoulder. But Cade wanted to be a part of her life regardless.

He trudged over to her and hugged her to him. "Let's get you back inside the cabin," he said. "You're getting too cold out here."

He glanced over at Terry, who nodded. "I'll be up in a minute," his friend said. "Need some coffee to warm my bones."

Leah followed him to the cabin where it all started. He took off his gloves and rubbed his hands in the direction of the fire, as did she.

"So what happens to the cabin now?"

"I guess someone should find Devon's daughter—or her child—"

Terry burst through the door. "I got something!"

Cade stiffened, unsure if any of them was ready to see what was inside the firesafe box that Terry held with gloved hands. He set it on

he table and, after removing his winter gloves,
e put on latex gloves. Terry pulled a camera
rom his pocket.

"Took pictures of it outside in the ground, too."
Ie handed the camera over to Cade. "Hold on to
hat. Take pictures as you see fit."

Cade chuckled. He wasn't sure this was how
hings should go down, but they had a chance,
 break in the weather, and they took it. Leah
eeded closure, and so did Cade.

Terry worked the lock and opened the lid. For
 minute they all stared at the files and papers.
More sludge to go through.

"May I?" Leah asked.

Terry frowned. "Put on gloves first."

After doing so, she flipped through the files
nd papers. "Tim's attorney notes on his clients
hat weren't convicted but that subsequently died
n accidents. As I'd thought. But what's this?"
he held up a recording device.

The three of them listened as Tim informed
Snyder of his discoveries. They heard Snyder
ll but confess to Tim why he'd done what he'd
lone, as though he could convince Tim that he'd
lone the right thing. And he mentioned another
ame: Marlow.

The detective who had disappeared.

Terry got on his sat phone to tell his higher-
ps about their discovery.

Leah appeared to buckle and Cade helped he
into a chair. She pressed her face into her hands
"It's over now. It's all over. But Tim should neve
have told Snyder what he'd been planning. Tha
cost him his life. Why would he do that?" Sh
looked at Cade as though she hoped he woul
have an answer for her.

"Maybe he wanted to give the detective
chance to turn himself in. He wanted him t
know that he'd turned into a criminal. Perhap
he hoped he would open Snyder's eyes to hi
crimes."

That was all Cade had, but he knew it fe
short. She was right. Doing that had cost Tim hi
life. He thought back to his father. Now he knev
the quarrel he had with Devon Hemphill. For ob
vious reasons, Devon had hated his father, an
maybe his father had wanted forgiveness. He'
obviously seen the errors of his ways and turne
his back on Devon's daughter for the sake of hi
marriage, but what Cade didn't know was if hi
father had turned his back on the child he'd fa
thered with her. None of it mattered now. His fa
ther had risked his life for the man, and had die
to save him, in spite of the animosity betwee
them. Cade might never know the full truth o
the rest of it unless he found Regina or her chil

When Leah said nothing, Cade lifted he
chin. "Sounds like your boss was a good mar

e didn't like having to turn in a detective like
at, and wanted to do the right thing. Give Sny-
er a chance."

She nodded, a smile growing in her supple
ps. Her vivid blue-greens locked on him. "And
ou're a good man, too, Cade. A man I don't
ant to lose. I never told you this. I'm sorry it
ok me so long…"

Cade frowned. Would she ever say it? "Tell
e."

"I love you. Thank you for waiting for me to
ay those words back to you."

He scooped her into his arms and crushed his
ps against hers, feeling her passion and love for
im. Then he released her. "Marry me, Leah.
ou don't know how long I've wanted to ask
ou this. I've been waiting until…until you said
e words or we found the box, whichever came
rst, and they happened together."

She laughed. He loved her laugh. Could listen
o it until death parted them.

"Well? Are you going to make me wait on this
nswer, too?"

"No, Cade."

His heart tanked.

"No more waiting. I want to marry you as
oon as possible. I've seen how quickly life can
e snuffed out. I don't want to waste another
inute living without you. I love you so much."

"Tell me how much." He was the one need
ing reassurances this time. But he knew the
chances of survival were better than good.

\* \* \* \* \*

ear Reader,

*uried* is the first book in a new series set in
laska, and I'm so glad you've joined me on
hat I hope will be an exciting adventure. When
first began my research on mountain search and
scue, I had no idea what kind of individuals
ade up a SAR team. I learned they are people
ho are willing to give up a good portion of their
ves to help others. People who are volunteers
d participate in training operations, and search
d rescue, all at their own expense. They are
perheroes—they don't get paid, either! They
e people who risk their lives. They are true
roes in every sense of the word.

I've read so many intense rescue stories about
ep sacrifices made that I could write about
arch and rescue for many years to come. And
ho knows? Maybe I'll do just that, because who
esn't love a hero?

In *Buried,* you met Cade and Leah, two in-
nse, strong and selfless people. Cade is all
out doing his best and doing what's right. He
ought he was following in the footsteps of his
eatest hero, his father. Then he learns that his
ther wasn't the man Cade thought. He was
ly human, after all. Leah has known all along
at men often touted as heroes have their own

secrets. In the end, the only One any of us c
look up to, the only True Hero, is Jesus Chris

He, too, volunteered Himself. He went wi
ingly to the cross and gave the ultimate sacrifi

I love to hear from my readers. Please visit r
website, www.elizabethgoddard.com, to lea
about how you can connect with me.

I pray many blessings on you!
*Elizabeth Goddard*

# Questions for Discussion

. Before the story starts, Leah witnesses a murder committed by the town hero—a detective whom everyone knows and loves. Someone who is charged to serve and protect. Someone people count on to solve crimes. Have you ever witnessed someone do something so completely out of character that no one would believe you if you told them? Discuss.

. Considering the circumstances, do you think Leah was right to find a safe place to stay while she figured out her next move rather than go straight to the authorities? Why or why not? What would you have done differently, if anything? Discuss possible flaws in your plan.

. The story starts with Leah running from Snyder, and the only place she has to run is into an avalanche danger zone. Do you think she should have turned and faced him instead of running? Why or why not?

. If for some reason, you feared for your life and could hide in an off-grid cabin in Alaska, do you feel you would be equipped to handle the experience and hardships? Why or why

not? Or would you have gone on the crui[se]
instead and taken your chances?

5. Cade has devoted his life to assessing av[a-]
lanche dangers to save lives. He's devoted h[is]
life to search and rescue missions to do t[he]
same. Do you know anyone who devotes [so]
much time to helping others? Discuss.

6. When Cade saves Leah from the avalanch[e,]
pulling her from the snow, there's som[e-]
thing about her that causes him to instant[ly]
connect with her—something he can't p[ut]
into words. Have you ever met anyone th[at]
you instantly liked or felt a deep conne[c-]
tion with? Discuss what happened. Did y[ou]
continue on with your relationship? Are y[ou]
still friends?

7. Because Cade connected with Leah [so]
quickly, he was able to sense on a deep lev[el]
that something was wrong, and he wasn't t[he]
kind of person who would let someone [go]
when he knew they needed help. What d[o]
you think about his attempts to stay involv[ed]
in her life and keep her safe? What do y[ou]
think of the family mantra, "Do not withho[ld]
good from those who deserve it, when it is [in]
your power to act." Proverbs 3:27?

. Leah held back the truth about what was going on from Cade because she feared for his life and the lives of his family if he knew too much. She hoped she could find out what she needed to without involving him any more than necessary, and in a way, that's what Tim, her boss had done to her. Have you ever kept a secret from someone to protect them? Do you understand her actions? Discuss.

# LARGER-PRINT BOOKS!

## GET 2 FREE
## LARGER-PRINT NOVELS
## PLUS 2 FREE
## MYSTERY GIFTS

*Love Inspired®*

## SUSPENSE

RIVETING INSPIRATIONAL ROMAN

### Larger-print novels are now available...